A BULLET FOR JESUS

I was so blessed to read this wonderful book by my friend Jim Boyd! This novel shows that like Jacob in the Bible, one can "wrestle" with God and God will answer your prayer. God loves to hear our cry for help.

—**Lee Allen Jenkins** / Pastor, Author, Speaker /
Eagles Nest Church / Roswell, GA

This is an addictive story of fear, surprise, romance, relationships, and strong faith that could only have been written by someone who had lived it. It's based on the real experiences of a naive, but highly motivated, young man who was dropped into a dangerous life or death inner-city gang world to execute an impossible mission.

—**Loren Burke** / Retired IBM Executive / Roswell, GA

This novel is an incredible example of the power of God to change lives and bring hope.

—**William Millliken** / Founder, Vice Chairman Communities in School / Author "The Last Dropout" / Arlington, VA

As followers of Christ, at times we are faced with challenges that shake us to our core, while testing the strength of the foundation of our faith.

In *A Bullet for Jesus*, Jim Boyd provides us with an insightful view of the wrestling within our souls when life takes us along a path that is less than ideal.

As the story of this novel unfolds, we discover the unwavering faithfulness of our Heavenly Father, who is able to redeem us even out of bleakest of situations.

—**Pastor Jonathan Booth** / Pastor/
Eagles Nest Church / Roswell, GA

Pastor Jim taps in the mystery question…Why do bad things happen to good people… Ecclesiastes 7:15 says, "There is a righteous man who perishes in his righteousness, and there is a wicked man who prolongs his life in his evildoing". Sometimes in our obedience we must take a bullet for Jesus… I recommend you read this book for your spiritual growth.

—**Phil Mckinnely** / Men's Ministry Leader / Eagles Nest Church / Roswell, GA

A
BULLET
FOR
JESUS

JIM BOYD

New York

A BULLET FOR JESUS

Published in New York, New York, by Morgan James Publishing. Morgan James and The Entrepreneurial Publisher are trademarks of Morgan James, LLC. www.MorganJamesPublishing.com

The Morgan James Speakers Group can bring authors to your live event. For more information or to book an event visit The Morgan James Speakers Group at www.TheMorganJamesSpeakersGroup.com.

A **free** eBook edition is available with the purchase of this print book.

CLEARLY PRINT YOUR NAME ABOVE IN UPPER CASE

Instructions to claim your free eBook edition:
1. Download the BitLit app for Android or iOS
2. Write your name in **UPPER CASE** on the line
3. Use the BitLit app to submit a photo
4. Download your eBook to any device

ISBN 978-1-63047-515-4 paperback
ISBN 978-1-63047-516-1 eBook
Library of Congress Control Number:
2014921195

Cover Design by:
Rachel Lopez
www.r2cdesign.com

Interior Design by:
Bonnie Bushman
bonnie@caboodlegraphics.com

In an effort to support local communities and raise awareness and funds, Morgan James Publishing donates a percentage of all book sales for the life of each book to Habitat for Humanity Peninsula and Greater Williamsburg.

Get involved today, visit
www.MorganJamesBuilds.com

Peninsula and
Greater Williamsburg
Building Partner

Dedicated to

Bill Milliken
Founder and Vice Chairman
Communities in Schools
This book is a gift from the author
Bill is my friend and mentor
He taught me to love the unloved

Even as the gun was pointed directly at him, his face remained peaceful... and then he said 'bless them.' He was executed right in front of me—because he was a Christian.

—From the book *Jesus Freaks* by Voice of the Martyrs

"When Christ Bids Us Come; He Bids Us Come and Die."
—*Dietrich Bonheoffer* (Reflections on Luke 14:25-33)

A young man with high spiritual values jeopardizes his very life while trying to help those caught up in a world of drugs and violence. What he encounters though will not only change his life, but put his very faith at risk.

"But Joey isn't there some other way? I didn't give up all I had and come here just to let some 'punk' gang leader kill me? Must my whole life and dreams be shattered by a bullet?"

"Well Jim, there's the door; you can either go out, turn left, walk down to the corner, face Eddie, and see if he really intends on killing you; or you can turn right and run for your life, hoping he doesn't catch you. Either way, your life and ministry here are probably over. You must decide whether to stay and fight for those you love or run away to live another day. No one can make that decision for you, not even me."

A Bullet for Jesus is based on a real story, mine. A faced paced thriller filled with danger, romance, joy and tragedy. I had the honor of living among these gangsters while serving God.

This privilege almost cost me my life.

It is a rare thing for one man to give his life for another; few have had the courage to do it.

—Romans 5:7

Acknowledgement

Many thanks to Angie at Spit-Seed for her and her staff professionally editing my manuscript. A professional Editor is very necessary to a "polished" novel.

I want to thank Terry Whalin, Acquisitions Editor, for Morgan James Publishing for choosing my manuscript and working closely with me to get it accepted.

Margo Toulouse and her team at Morgan James have been very patient with me and extremely helpful in guiding me through the publishing industry. Without the guidance of everyone, my novel would have just remained on paper.

THANK YOU

I thank my family and friends for their patience and helpful suggestions.

For my wife, JoEllen Boyd for the countless hours she put in typing and re-typing my manuscript. Her insightful finding of mistakes I made kept my manuscript looking professional.

My son, Jim Boyd, daughters Ashley Barlow and Cara Sadira constantly gave me encouragement to "keep at it" during the many months and years needed to produce my novel. My good friend Alecia Brooks who was the first to read my manuscript and enthusiastically tell me I must publish it.

INTRODUCTION

Every day the newspapers explode with the tragic headlines of another teen killing innocent people. Teen violence today is one of the worst tragedies America has ever experienced, and it is one of the hardest and the easiest to correct. I will show you one approach that can hopefully end teen violence.

New York City is a city of contradictions: alive by day and dangerous by night. Even in the nicest neighborhoods, you can be faced with a crazed drug addict who will kill you to get the money he needs to buy more drugs. Life, your life, means nothing to some of the most hardened teen criminals stalking the big cities of America.

Are we to remain victims of this cancer? Where is God in all of this?

Many of the teen criminals come from the projects located all over the city. The projects consist of old dilapidated, tall, drab-colored government apartment buildings, many as tall as forty-two stories with just four taking up a whole city block. Inside of this block live thousands of often desperate people jammed into small apartments with no air conditioning and the oppressive heat rising up into their rooms at night. With not enough space for a family of five to six people, they often share beds or sleep on the floor. Sometimes they even go up to the roof to sleep or just go outside to roam the streets looking for trouble.

Many are a people without hope. Their educational dreams are usually destroyed by an inept system before they reach the ninth grade, and many of them fail out. Jobs are scarce, and the future looks horrible. Welfare is often their only salvation, drugs their only escape from this ugly reality. Gangs form within each city block to protect one another and occasionally to attack, rob, or kill one another. One wrong word or look could accidently lead to violence. Each person carries a sense of despondency and arrogance. This leads to an atmosphere of extreme violence.

Into this nightmare and deadly life, God called a young man, Joey Jones, to live among these outcasts and show them as well as teach them that there is a God, and that He knows of their hurts, frustrations, and fears. Joey wanted to bring light into this darkness. It was not an easy assignment, but a challenge that Joey accepted.

The question was; how he, a white man, would be received into this often-violent community of blacks and Hispanics, many of whom saw the white man as the cause of all their misery. Would he last a day? A week? A month? Only time would tell.

Four years later God called me, another white man, to walk alongside Joey and hopefully to bring more of God's love to the city's unloved, those whom the "good people" of society only pray they will never encounter.

The summer I arrived was particularly hot and oppressive. One spark, one wrong look, one police car passing by could easily set off an incident of violence that could end with several people getting hurt.

This is a story about Young Life in New York City as told by one who lived through it. It is a story of love and danger of hope and tragedy of miracles of God

WHAT? OH NO!
YOU READY TO DIE PUNK?

Turning to face me, an angry black man swung his large knife from one side of him to the other. "Are you talking to me, white man? Just who do you think you are?"

While walking back from visiting some of my new Puerto Rican friends in the Alfred Smith projects, I heard a loud commotion and saw a large crowd only a hundred feet ahead of me. I quickly ran to see what was going on. As I neared, I heard someone crying in a loud voice. "Please, please don't kill me, mister, I was only funning you. Please, oh please God, don't let him kill me."

When I quickly pushed my way to the front of the crowd, I saw a tall young black man wearing a dirty white T-shirt and cut-off jeans, his scraggly hair flying and sweat pouring down his face as he chased an older black man around and around a shiny old Cadillac that had been propped up on cinder blocks. All of its wheels were missing, most likely stolen.

A large crowd of maybe fifty people stood laughing at the old man. My heart went out to the poor fellow. I recognized him as one of the neighborhood drunks. The old man had on no shoes or shirt. Each man was slowly circling the car. The young man kept lunging across the car, trying to cut the older man.

In horror, I watched for a moment, hoping someone would rescue the old man, but no one did. They just all laughed. How could they be so cruel? Life seemed to be so meaningless here. People died all the time, sometimes violently.

Stepping forward, I said, "Okay, you've had your fun, now leave the old man alone."

Abruptly he stopped chasing the old man, turned toward me, and began to scream and cuss at me. As quickly as he could, he closed the gap between us, slashing his knife from side to side. "Who do you think you are talking to, Whitey? I'm going to gut you from end to end. Even your momma won't recognize you when I am done."

Spinning on my heels, I ran away as fast as I could. I had not expected him to turn on me. I tried to run around the crowd back to my apartment where I would be safe. What incredibly bad timing I had; a truck pulled right in front of me forcing me to run in a different direction. I ran into the nearest alley, only to have it end within a few feet.

With nowhere to turn, I faced death as it raced towards me.

I froze!

I could not believe myself. I had faced danger before, but I could not think!

All of my hand-to-hand combat training in the army left me. I stood there paralyzed with fear.

Kick out at him, I thought. *Kick him where it hurts!*

But nothing happened; my leg didn't move.

I knew I was about to die at the hands of a crazy man, and none of my friends, here or back home, would ever know why. Tears began streaming down my cheeks.

The man stopped just a few inches from me, so close I could smell the alcohol on his breath. He leaned in nose to nose.

"Coward, get out of my sight, white man. Go back to wherever you came from!"

As he turned to walk away, another disaster happened. Abruptly, my bladder gave way, and I could feel hot pee pouring down my leg. What a mess I was, tears mingled with snot flowing freely down my face and hot pee flowing down my leg. *Oh God, what a miserable failure I am.*

I limped out of the alley to the sound of hoots and catcalls. *Oh God, now what? If only I can make it back to my apartment without anyone I know seeing me.* Pee squished out of my sneakers as I slowly walked home.

I had only been living in New York City and working with Young Life a couple of months. Already I was a failure.

The short walk to my apartment, only a couple of blocks away, turned into one of the longest walks of my life.

Pushing open the door to my apartment, I quickly took off my pants and threw them into the shower, washed my body and collapsed onto my bunk. I was so discouraged. Soon I was fast asleep.

"Jim, what in the world are you doing in bed?" Joey shouted as he rattled my bunk bed. "Get up and get out there with your gang. I'm not paying you to sleep!"

Paying me? I thought. *I'm a volunteer, and I quit.*

Rising slowly, I shook my head to clear it. "But Joey, you don't understand."

Leaning down into my face, he said, "No, I don't, and I don't want to hear another word."

With that, he slammed the door and left.

I cried softly and prayed, *Oh God, what am I going to do?*

New York City is the land of dreams and hopes. Many young people come here looking to find fame. Some find only trouble. I too came here, but for an entirely different reason. I felt I was following God's call to a new and exciting ministry.

I had just left my life as a college student in Washington, DC, where I was also the leader of our college group at my church. I was following what I believed was a call from God to come here and help Young Life rescue those who were trapped in a cycle of violence.

This city is also known for its unimaginable level of sudden violence.

I had high hopes of being able to make a difference in the lives of others.

What I experienced was that sometimes in following God, one must be prepared to die. I always thought this meant to die to certain temptations or beliefs, not *actually die*. That was for missionaries in distant countries, not here in the United States.

"Take up your cross and follow me" had only been a saying to me, but now I would find that just like Jesus, I might not only have to carry my cross, but I might have to die on it.

Never did I expect to find so much danger, or to one day face death itself at the hands of a drunken killer.

PART ONE

CHAPTER 1

As I followed the directions on the map, I soon entered a totally different part of this famous city from what I had ever imagined. It looked horrible. Even some of the worst scenes of destruction from war movies paled in comparison.

I had never seen so much filth and trash, and actually, I thought I was in the wrong place.

The more I drove, the more I agonized over my decision to come here.

As I approached the address where Young Life was headquartered, I realized that I was entering a land unlike any I had ever experienced before. The street channeled into a corridor of extremely tall buildings. Trash littered the street as well as the sidewalk, and each building looked just like the last one. I felt like I was entering a prison. I was scared, but that was just the beginning.

I saw that there were two buildings side by side with two more behind. Together they took up the entire block. They were tall and blocked out the sun, maybe forty stories high. Large rats the size of cats ran in and out of the trash. The area gave me a sense of hopelessness and violence.

Huddled together on every corner were small groups of black men drinking and laughing. They stared menacingly at me as I drove slowly by. Who could I dare to ask for help if I wasn't in the right neighborhood? Perhaps my map was wrong, or I had misunderstood the directions.

A large dog came racing out from one of the groups as I passed by; I floored the gas pedal. Hoping against hope that I was in the wrong spot, I looked for a place to turn around when I saw a faded, dirty logo that frightened me. In the window of a small three-story apartment building, the sign read:

215 East Madison Street—Young Life Office

I screamed so loud in my car, I was afraid the windows would burst. *No, No, Lord, this can't be true!*

Having found the address listed in the book and looked for a place to park. The spaces alongside both curbs were taken.

Every fourth car was jacked up, sitting on cinder blocks with no tires, no wheels, hood up, engine missing, and the windows busted out. Shattered glass from car windows littered the street.

Where should I park? Would my car be stolen or destroyed before I returned?

Two blocks away, I found a spot in front of a post office with a sign that read *15-Minute Parking Only*. Hurriedly, I walked back toward the Young Life address.

Arriving at 215 Madison Street, I paused. Now, I was very frightened.

Sitting on the steps leading to the front door was a man puking out his guts. The strong smell of alcohol rushed toward me. I felt as if I was suffocating.

The man looked up at me and roared, "What are you looking at?"

After he had finished puking, the drunk stood, and it looked like he was going to rush down the stairs and destroy me. Without thinking, I recoiled and took a couple of steps back. For a moment, I wondered if I'd made a big mistake and should get back into my car and drive away.

Just then the door to the building flew open and two guys walked out. Seeing me, they stopped. "You must be Jim," one said.

Startled, I stammered, "Yeah."

"Joey asked us to keep an eye out for you; come on in."

Eying the mean-looking drunk on the steps in front of me, I hesitated. The man now stared at me with fire in his eyes.

Sensing my fear, one of the fellows turned to the drunk and shouted, **"Get out of here!"**

Shifting his stance, he looked up at the two young men, then got up and left. He glared at me as he walked past. I was still shaking with fear when one of them came down the steps and introduced himself.

"I'm Frankie," said the slender, deeply tanned man. "Come with me."

I followed Frankie inside and immediately was overpowered by the stench of urine. It felt nauseated. Later I learned that men who had to pee came into the narrow hallway, urinated against the wall, and walked out. A pool of fresh urine lay along the wall.

I could hear loud voices arguing inside one of the apartment. As we passed another, loud Latin music filtered out through the open door. All the way at the end of the hallway was a single door. Frankie opened it, and inside sat some young men.

The one white guy in the apartment stood and smiled warmly. "You must be Jim. Welcome. I'm Joey."

Hesitantly I walked in. Joey was surrounded by several young black and Hispanic men. I still wasn't sure where I was or what was going to happen next.

Joey walked toward me and extended his hand.

He was taller than I expected, standing possibly five feet ten inches to six feet with thick, wavy black hair and a smile that lit up his whole face. Instantly, I felt better.

Wearing faded blue jeans, a white T-shirt, and white sneakers, Joey looked a lot like the college friends I had just left. This helped to put me at ease.

I felt better seeing all the big black guys sitting in a circle. I hoped I would be working with them. They reminded of the guys I had worked with in DC. Someone offered me a seat and I nervously stammered, "Thank you,"

Everyone burst out laughing. I was sure I must have blushed or something.

"It's okay, white boy," a voice called out. "Just have a seat."

The only seat was next to a huge black fellow with a large tattoo on his arm wearing a sleeveless T-shirt. He was much older than the others and looked like a really bad dude. I hesitated.

The man said, "I don't bite—really. My name is Jimmy."

I sat next to him and smiled faintly.

Then Joey introduced the rest. "Jim, this is Gee, Clarkie, Little Eddie, Caesar, and you already met Frankie. Don't worry; you'll get to know us all."

"Where you from?" Gee asked.

I remember answering with a squeaky voice. "DC."

Jimmy reached over with a big hand that looked like it belonged to a boxer and offered to shake my puny white hand.

Once I shook Jimmy's hand and felt the love transmitted through that warm handshake, I immediately felt better. My fears relaxed. This must be the place—and God must be in it.

"Jim." Joey gestured toward the man next to Frankie. "This is Caesar, one of our best contacts with the Puerto Ricans."

"Caesar," Joey said, chuckling, "as you can see, Jim's new to the area and just a little unsure that God has really called him here."

Most of the guys laughed.

"Jim wants to help people, so I'm assigning you to take care of him."

Caesar looked at me and gave a warm and loving grin. "Sure thing, Joey."

Caesar was shorter than I and well built, probably five feet six with a tiny goatee and sparkling brown eyes. He had a small mustache and kept twisting the ends into curls. He walked with a swagger, his left hand in his pocket.

Slowly I rose and followed Caesar out the door.

Immediately the powerful stench of pee overwhelmed me.

Wait a minute, God. Where are we going? Please don't tell me this is where I will be living.

My heart felt lost and broken.

"So, what's a smart guy like you from Washington, DC, doing here?"

"It's sort of a long story, but I read this book about the great work God had going on here in New York, and…."

"…and He sent you here?" Caesar laughed. "Here? Man, either God doesn't like you, or you did something that really ticked Him off. Well, here's where we stay."

I had just followed Caesar down a narrow hallway and up a flight of stairs when the powerful smell of urine engulfed me, burning my nose and eyes.

Caesar turned and smiled. "Don't worry, Jim. You'll get used to it. I did." He led me to a door at the end of the hallway.

When Caesar opened the door, the first thing I saw was cockroaches. They swarmed across the sink and up the walls. The apartment had a small living room with a dirty broken couch, a microwave on a stand, a sink and a bathroom with a shower. There was also a small back room with two double bunk beds. The walls were bare and the paint was peeling. The room had one light bulb.

Caesar pointed to one of the lower bunk beds. "You sleep here." The bunks were jammed against a wall. There were two small windows, one at the foot of each bed.

Each window had bars rusted in place. No one was getting in or out. The windows had been painted shut years ago.

Caesar pulled out a drawer in a small dresser. "Put your stuff in here."

"Tell me about yourself, Caesar."

"Later, maybe when I get to know you better. All you need to know for now…." He paused and laughed. "All you need to know for now is that I'm the best-looking Puerto Rican you'll ever meet."

Caesar left, and I sat down on my newly assigned bunk.

"Don't worry Jim; you'll get used to it."

Used to this? Oh, God! Help me!

CHAPTER 2

Joey sent for me. "Jim, I don't know much about you, and in a minute, I would like for you to tell me more, but based on the information I received from the Young Life people you worked with in Washington, DC, I am assigning you to work with the Puerto Ricans. They're a good bunch, but their leader is a fellow named Eddie, and he is a bad character. He can be nice and funny, or he can be mean and hurt someone bad, even kill when he chooses. This is a very touchy situation. The Puerto Ricans ran off the last guy I assigned to work with them, and when I say ran off, I mean they chased him clear back to his home in Ohio. They can be very dangerous, very quickly."

He paused and watched for my reaction. My face must have revealed my panic. *Puerto Ricans? But I don't know any Spanish. Oh, God!*

"Tell me why you came to this particular work?" Joey asked.

"Well, first of all, there was a night at a Young Life weekend where my life was radically changed. You see, I had always been a good kid, a 'religious' guy, but one night I was challenged by a dynamic speaker to take a good look at myself. That night, I gave my heart and my life to Jesus, and I have never looked back. I fell so in love with God. I have spent my whole life ever since serving Jesus. I am sold out to follow Him wherever He leads me.

"The reason I'm here is God stirred up a fire in my heart—a passion to come here and help. I prayed about it for weeks. I asked God, 'Why should I give up all that I have and go to New York City?' I was a leader in my college-age group, in a very large and prestigious church. A lot of very pretty girls thought that I was really something special, and I had a lot of friends on campus. I had it made; everyone loved me.

"I asked God, 'Should I leave it all to work with hoodlums, people I don't even know, far off in New York City?'"

"Despite all my questions, God prevailed. I finally gave in. I prayed, 'If this is what you want, Lord, then I'll do it, but you got to help me—I'm afraid.'" After that, the excitement just began to build.

"I don't know what I have to offer, and I was surprised at the neighborhood around here. In Washington, DC, I lived in a nice apartment and visited the guys I worked with at Young Life, but I didn't live with them. The neighborhood seemed a whole lot safer than this one. Honestly, this neighborhood scares me. I don't know that I can live here—I don't know that I like it here. Maybe I made a big mistake and should just go home."

"Yeah, I know what you mean," Joey said. "I too left everything behind at the suggestion of my pastor and came here. At first, I was kinda lonely and felt out of place. Being the only white man had its advantages and disadvantages; the women loved me, and the guys hated me." Joey laughed.

His dark eyes sparkled, and he arched his eyebrows in mock surprise. Sitting back and putting his hands behind his head, he just chuckled. "Now that I've been here five years, I know I made the right decision. So many lives have been changed! Also, we have a solid group of committed

Christians now. I too was very scared when I arrived. Truthfully, there is a lot of violence and danger here.

"I believe that you'll be all right—but *only you* can make that decision. Pray about it."

"Has anyone heard from Jim?'

"As a matter of fact, Phil, I have, just yesterday," Tom replied.

"I hate to admit it, but I am worried about him. New York City is no picnic. I really was not sure he should have left us here in Washington, DC."

"I know what you mean, Phil. He is not a hardened type of person. As you know, he is a very gentle soul."

"I also talked to Joey Jones; he seems to feel that despite Jim's doubts, he will be just fine. He is assigning two of his best men, Frankie and Caesar, to watch over him. Jim sounded a little shaky on the phone. Said he never saw such a filthy neighborhood, and his apartment is a nightmare, a *real* nightmare."

"Thanks, Tom. I guess that we all need to keep Jim in prayer. I don't know that I could do what he is doing. Maybe I'm just too old or too chicken. Beside, my wife would hate me if Jim was killed or something really bad happened to him. She was not in favor of him going."

"Joey, I've told you about me; please tell me about yourself—where you came from and how you came to here and why."

"Funny thing, Jim, I come from Pennsylvania just like you." Joey laughed. "Maybe, it's a good place to start life, ya think?" Again he laughed.

"Well I think the Lord sent me here, because in many ways, I'm just like the people we minister to. They quit school; I quit school. I was an angry young teenager. I had no direction—just sort of wandering through life, waiting for something good to happen or maybe get a job in the steel mills. Ever worked in a mill, Jim?"

Laughing, I replied, "Yeah, for three days."

"What happened? Get fired?"

"Yeah." I snickered. "I got caught playing jokes on an old man, a DP." (These initials always stood for a displaced person, an immigrant, or a Dumb Pollock as we used to say in those days). "Well, he was both. He spoke no English. One day when I got there early, I took an out-of-order sign and placed it on his machine."

Laughing, Joey asked, "And then what happened?"

I sat back in my chair and laughed. "Then he came in, saw the sign, and ran to get the foreman. Soon he came back with the foreman and showed him the sign. The foreman took one look at the sign and glared over at me; he walked to the sign, pulled it off, and clicked the machine to start. It started immediately, of course, and then he walked over to me and shouted above my machine's noise. "You think you are pretty funny, don't you? Don't you realize that if that man's machine no work, he no work?" Pointing to the old man, he said, "Him, I need. You, I no need. Get out of here."

"So, that was it, no more jobs in the mills?"

"Nah, no more for me. I was only working there for a couple of months while waiting to go into the army."

"Joey, were you in the Army?"

"As it turned out, I never served in the military at all. Anyway, one day I met a very strange man. Up 'til this point, nobody really cared much for me, except a few of my friends from the local pool hall. One day this guy walked in and just sat around watching me play pool, and I got to wondering what his game was. Well, he challenged me to a game, and of course I beat him. We played a couple more then he left. Next day he was back. After a few games between us, I asked him why an older dude like him was hanging out in a pool hall. He said 'I came to meet you.' So we went over to the counter and he bought me a drink, and we talked. I thought maybe he had a job for me; after all I am big, strong, and mighty handsome." Joey did his famous act of wiggling his eyebrows up and down to make me laugh.

"Well," I said, "at least you are big," and then I laughed.

"Yeah, and still better looking than most. Well, he started telling me about a ranch out in Colorado where they rode horses, and he said there were plenty of pretty girls. He even showed me some pictures. I had no idea where Colorado was, but if Colorado had all those pretty girls, I was going. The ranch was run by Young Life.

"When I arrived, I couldn't believe my eyes. I had never seen such beautiful country, and there we were way up high in the mountains. I swear that on some days, I could almost reach out and touch the clouds. I rode horses, ate breakfast at a campfire after a long trail ride, and actually got to gallop for a hundred yards on my horse. It was even fun getting up long before sunrise to saddle up my horse and ride off into the breaking dawn.

"Each day was filled with fun activities, and each night was a fun time and a short talk about the meaning of life from one of the leaders. When we went to our cabins to get some sleep, our cabin counselor had us talk about ourselves. At first, I was kinda quiet; didn't want anybody knowing my business. But as time went on, I learned that most of the kids in the camp were screwed up, just like me. The meals were so fantastic and there was so much food that in just one week, I gained ten pounds.

"Gradually I opened up during cabin talk time and shared about my loneliness and frustrations. On the last night there, I listened more closely as one of the leaders talked about what Jesus had done for us. Sometime later after returning home, I gave my heart to Jesus. It wasn't just the camp or the people there; it was that they loved me unconditionally, and no one else had ever done that for me." Joey's eyes moistened with tears as he remembered. Laughing as he wiped away some tears, he added, "I also learned you don't have to be a sissy to cry.

"Sometime later, I started attending some Young Life meetings in my area and began to grow in my relationship with the Lord. One thing led to another, and one day, here I was. You see, I knew God had a spot for me working with kids who were like me; kids who thought they had no hope, lived in a hopeless situation, and had resorted to drugs and violence as a means to cope. But I wondered if I could somehow show these kids that someone just like them, from the outside, could actually understand them and love them."

Getting up, Joey went into his kitchen and poured himself some coffee.

"Want some?"

"No thanks."

Coming back into the room and settling down in his favorite chair, Joey continued. "At first, it was weird being here—really weird. Friends helped me get set up, and some stayed awhile. But here I was, a very good-looking (arching his eyebrows) white man in an almost all black/Hispanic neighborhood. The women dug me, but the guys looked at me suspiciously. My main contact was the priest at St. Chris's church. We met for prayer, and he introduced me to several of his friends. But the one thing that really helped was that Young Life had already established another work uptown in Harlem. The leader of that work and I became really good friends.

"What made it really hard was my white skin. It took a lot of time playing basketball and just hanging around to build trust with these guys, as trust with most of them did not come easy. These guys were just like I had been, cold and hard in their feelings, alone and afraid of life.

Life for them could end violently at any time. I really had to trust the Lord to keep me safe and help me to love them, and to help them like me and respect me as an equal.

"Sometimes God calls us to do very difficult things, but He always gives us the strength. These guys came from violent backgrounds and would not have had any problem hurting or maybe even killing me. 'Yea, though I walk through the valley of the shadow of death' became one of my mantras."

"Joey, why have you stayed all these years?"

"Because these guys are worth it."

"Can you tell me how they came to trust you?"

"Well, that you will have to find out for yourself by learning how to build your own relationship with the Puerto Ricans. Two things you need to know; one is spending enough time and waiting. Relationships are what it is all about. Secondly, don't screw up what has taken me so long to build. Frankie and Caesar are great guys, but they are not perfect, and they may not fit your mold of what a Christian is supposed to act or be like. Time to go, Jim, lots of work to be done."

CHAPTER 3

There were four different gangs in the area, the Blacks, the Puerto Ricans, the Italians, and the Chinese. The Blacks and the Puerto Ricans lived in the same project. My assigned group, the Puerto Ricans, loved to sing and party.

The projects were government-housing apartments for people on welfare. The Alfred E. Smith Apartments was one of these. Located between the Manhattan and Brooklyn Bridges, they covered an entire city block. This is where the group I would be working with lived.

The grass that had been planted between the buildings had long since worn out, and now there was only mud. There were no flowers and only a few small trees.

Thousands of people lived in each building. The complex had a reputation of being so violent that the police rarely came into it.

Every Friday night the apartments were filled with partying. The air was filled with the smell of alcohol and loud Puerto Rican music.

For the Puerto Rican men, rule *numero uno* was that you could dance or mess with any girl at the party except their sisters and cousins.

Problem was, every woman there was somebody's sister or cousin. It wasn't long before somebody started to shout, "I told you to leave my cousin alone!" This was usually followed by a few shots fired into the air and everybody screaming as they tried to fight their way out of the apartment.

Most would go downstairs and outside. Some would go to one of the benches where they would gather and make beats and sing. The music was made by tapping a pen or knife on an empty can or bottle.

The smaller the object, the higher the note. Some would tap the bench with a stick. Somehow, it all came together in a Latin rhythm. It took me a while to learn enough Spanish to understand some of the songs. At first, I just stood there and tapped my foot.

Oh God, I've got so much to learn …help me to love these people … help me to lead them to you. I've seen some violent things; please protect me, especially as I walk home in the dark.

Three months after I arrived, Frankie, Caesar, and I went to a local gym where two boxers were sparring. What an experience! I'd never been to a live boxing ring.

One of the boxers was taking a brutal beating. He had several cuts on his face and blood dripping down from one eye. The other boxer pounded on him unmercifully. It hurt me just to watch him. He kept getting knocked down, but he always got up again. *Such courage*, I mused. Finally, he sat there on the floor for a moment, blood mingled with sweat oozing down his face from both eyes, and then he got up, took off his gloves, and climbed unsteadily out of the ring.

Wow, that must really hurt.

The winning boxer put his hands over his head and strutted around like a proud rooster, his head bobbing back and forth, arms bent with his elbows partly behind his back. "I am the champ!" he roared. "I am the **CHAMP**! Anyone else dare to challenge me?" I shook my head and laughed inwardly. Who would be fool enough to go into the ring with that violent man?

A voice somewhere behind me said, "Put Jim in." My knees instantly sank.

Turning to my right, I saw a tall, well-built, dark young man with a worn blue baseball cap tilted to one side. Despite whoever this guy was, I was not going into that ring.

"What? No thanks." I smiled. "Not me. No thanks."

Instantly, several hands lifted me off my feet as if following a command.

Struggling, I braced myself. *No—I can't go into the ring—how humiliating it will be. I've never been in a fight in my life. What if this guy really pounds me like he did the last fellow?*

I was supposed to be a leader; I couldn't let this happen. All my struggling was in vain. Several hands lifted me up and into the ring. *Oh God, help me!*

Held tightly in place in the ring, I came face to face with the young Puerto Rican boxer who had just devastated his foe. I could feel gloves being slipped over my hands as the bell rang.

There I was, suddenly facing this semi-pro.

What do I do, Lord?

Without any warning, a bright blinding light burst through my eyes and sent me spinning backward into the ropes.

My head pounded with pain. Quickly, I took a few steps sideways. My vision blurred, but I could still see.

Surprising myself I thought, *Whoa, I have just been hit, and hit hard, by this expert—maybe giving his best shot.*

And I'm not dead?

Praise God!

It was an exhilarating feeling. Immediately I began chasing this winner around the ring—pounding, not boxing, just swinging wildly and hitting him again and again until he fled out of the ring.

Sweat pouring down my face, my heart racing, I could barely breathe; suddenly I felt ecstatic.

I threw both hands wildly into the air above me.

Strutting around like the guy before me, I screamed, *"I am the champ, the undefeated champ!"* I had never felt like this before. Oh, what a feeling—like being the first person to fly.

I stood there triumphantly and raised my hands in victory.

The crowd hollered, *"Jim's the man, Jim's the man."*

I felt so good. This foray had not ended in disaster but in victory. *Thank you, Jesus!* I continued strutting around the ring just like the other guy. This only brought gales of laughter from everybody. I was so glad I did not embarrass Joey.

While I was taking off my gloves, the young man who had instigated the whole thing walked up to me. "My name is Eddie."

Well-built and handsome, he was taller than the rest and had his dark wavy hair plastered close to his head. His relaxed demeanor gave off an air of confidence, and his smile revealed his gentle soul. His eyes, though, were cold and steely. A scar ran down his cheek on the left side of his face, possibly from a knife cut. It ran close to his eye. From the look of Eddie, whoever did it most likely was not around anymore. His T-shirt fit his massive chest muscles tightly, and he had cut off the sleeves to show his massive arm muscles. He was definitely not a man to mess with.

Everyone seemed to really like Eddie. *"Hey guys,"* he roared, *"let's throw Jim a victory party."*

"Yeah, how 'bouts a pig roast?" someone shouted.

Eddie smiled and asked, "Jim, ever been to a Puerto Rican pig roast?"

Feeling like the champion they were proclaiming me to be, I swelled my chest with pride and strutted around again. "*No,*" I said loudly and with a really big grin. I was having the time of my life.

"Well, we are going to treat you to a royal pig roast," Eddie said. "Here's what we'll do. I'll call my cousin in Jersey. He has a big house, and we'll have it there. I'll get the pig and the apples. Since it takes several hours to roast the pig, everybody meet me here at four thirty in the morning, and my cousin will pick us up."

I headed back to my apartment, gloating all the way, to share the news with Joey. Me, Jim, from a small town in Pennsylvania, had beat the Puerto Ricans' champ, and now they were having a royal pig roast in my honor. *Now, Joey will be proud of me. Young Life wins again.*

I stopped by Scott's Deli, my favorite eating place. They always had great sandwiches. I particularly liked their double cheeseburgers. They just dripped of juice or fat; don't know which, and lots of ketchup. I loved washing it down with a thick chocolate milkshake.

Scott was a friendly guy that I had learned I could confide in sometimes. Scott didn't like the guys I hung out with but appreciated what I was doing for them.

Sometimes I started my day there and finished it there. Sometimes Scott would treat me to a cup of coffee. Scott's Deli was located on the corner just three houses from where I lived.

"Jim, I am so proud of you," Scott said. When he saw me come in, he left the kitchen and came over to where I sat. "Just don't mess it up. You get one chance with these guys, and only one. Be on time and you will make an important friend of Eddie. Something you need to know about Eddie—he can be a cold-hearted killer. He has hurt a lot of people. Sometimes he has to in order to protect his position as gang leader. This is a violent world down here, and where he lives in the Smith projects is especially violent. Three gangs live in the same project. A vicious fight could start anytime for any reason.

"Just be careful. If you have an appointment with Eddie, don't be late and don't blow it off. He won't forgive.

"Be late, and you might as well pack your bags and go back to all your friends in DC."

"Thanks for the advice, Scott. I won't let you down—no way!"

"What a beautiful morning!" I said after waking from a deep sleep. I stood and stretched then looked out the filthy window. I watched the rats devour a cat.

It suddenly dawned on me that the sun was up; it wasn't dark out as it usually was at such an early hour. "Oh, no," I wailed. "What happened to my alarm? Don't tell me I overslept and missed my own victory pig roast!"

I raced as fast I could down the ten blocks to the Smith projects and to the elevator in Eddie's building, hoping that someone was still around. I ran into Johnny, Eddie's younger brother, in the hallway.

"Johnny…." I gasped, my heart pounding from running ten blocks. "Is anybody left?"

"Left? Who you talking about?"

"Eddie—have you seen Eddie?"

"Eddie's in bed."

"What?" I couldn't believe my ears.

"I was supposed to meet Eddie and your cousin from Jersey at four thirty this morning."

"Cousin? What cousin? We ain't got no cousin in Jersey." Johnny gave a questioning stare. "Four thirty this morning? Man, somebody's putting you on." He laughed.

Putting me on?

It couldn't be.

Yesterday I was this big hero and ...today I was somebody's fool?

My heart was broken; I got a little mad. Eddie would pay for this! Barely able to walk, exhausted and tired, I retreated to my apartment, dropped into my bed and fell sound asleep.

Later that day, I went down to the projects. As I expected, Eddie and his whole gang were there.

Hurrying my step, I tried to look really flustered and sorry. "Eddie, I'm so sorry that I missed the pig roast this morning. My alarm didn't go off."

"Man, that's so bad. You missed the greatest party ever, and the guest of honor didn't even show up. Man, what are you, some kind of loser?"

Turning his back to me, Eddie winked when I looked at the others, but then he faced me again and said, "My cousin from Jersey drove all the way over here just for a celebration for you, and you didn't even have the courtesy to show up. Get away from me—loser."

"Come on, Eddie, lighten up," Johnny said. "After all, Jim's just a dumb white boy."

Everybody laughed, and then Eddie said, "Oh, it's OK; we had a really good party without you. Maybe next month we'll set another one up."

Walking toward me was one of the most beautiful women I had ever seen.

Her tan skin was flawlessly smooth, and the afternoon moisture from the humidity made her shoulders glow and reflect the beauty of the day.

She had on a tank top with a deep plunging neckline. Her body was magnificent.

There was gentleness to her face.

Somehow, she seemed so out of place here; this was a land of hopelessness and violence.

She, a precious beauty, seemed in need of a protector.

Over the next few weeks, I saw her everywhere I went.

Was this a coincidence, or a message from God?

Each time I saw her, my heart stopped.

She had such incredible beauty and grace.

Joy radiated from her sparkling dark eyes. They were so beautiful, and so seductive.

The short shorts she wore exposed her magnificent legs.

I wanted to take her in my arms and hold her—hold her close.

She was everything a red-blooded man could dream of or desire, but she was definitely off limits.

Eddie pointed her out on one occasion and said she was his sister Carmen. *Nobody* could touch her without Eddie's permission. Eddie protected her from all the guys.

Frankie had once told me that to go out on a date with a Puerto Rican girl was quite a ritual. First, you had to have her father's approval. Next, her mother or an aunt had to go along and walk between the two of you. No touching!

You could often get around this rule by having the mother or aunt close by while the two of you talked. Or you could go to the movies and sit together while Mom or Aunt sat a couple of rows away.

Once there, in the dark of the movie theater, you could hold hands, kiss, do some hugging, but that was all. Puerto Ricans took a serious view of their women. No one messed with them or talked to them without permission.

Every time I saw Carmen, a fire burned within me, a fire that burned more and more dangerously. Struggling with the concept that a good Christian leader should not think such thoughts, I wondered if I would someday burn in hell for the things I imagined.

I could not let my thoughts get out of control.

CHAPTER 4

E ddie and I were sitting on Eddie's bench. Eddie called out, "Hey, Sis, c'mere."

Slowly Carmen walked toward us.

"Jim, you know my sister Carmen? She ain't much, but she's all I got."

Eddie looked at Carmen. "Carmen, Jim's my new friend; he works with Joey, and he's here to help us. Be nice to him."

Carmen extended her hand and gave me a really big smile. "Any friend of Eddie's is a friend of mine …not!" She smirked. "Really, Jim, I wouldn't give the time of day for most of his friends, but you…." She shrugged her shoulders. "For a white boy, you're okay."

They both laughed.

Part of me was honored; part was offended.

If she did like me, it would be suicide to say so in front of her brother. We would have to meet secretly, and if anyone ever found out, we would be severely punished.

I had to learn to control my feelings and at the same time take any teasing they said about Carmen and me.

The desire to be alone with Carmen and get to know her grew stronger and stronger day by day.

"Carmen," Eddie blurted out. "So what do you really think of my friend Jim?"

"Jim's a jerk." She laughed. Carmen knew full well that if she had any feelings for me, she could not let on. On the other hand, maybe she really meant it.

Me a jerk? I hope not.

Carmen confided her feelings for me to her cousin Lena, whom everybody called Skamp, a play on the words she-tramp. Lena eventually told me that when Carmen first met me, she thought *maybe he really is different from the other guys. Most of the time, all the other guys want is sex. But Jim shows me respect. However, if Eddie ever finds out that his precious sister likes a guy, that will mean big trouble for the guy.*

Caesar had one time confided to me that although Eddie didn't know it, Carmen and Skamp were close. Skamp was Carmen's cousin on her mother's side.

Most of all Skamp was a drug addict and the neighborhood slut. She traded her body for drugs all the time. Skamp had once been pretty, but the ravages of drugs had changed her. Her long, blond hair was straight and unwashed. She wore the same clothes every day, and her arms and legs were filled with purple spots from needle marks where she had injected herself with drugs. To see her was to pass by and not even acknowledge her existence. To Eddie and his friends, she was a joke—a rotten joke.

Skamp was a year younger than Carmen.

Carmen was seventeen and in her last year of high school; she had no plans for what to do with her life once she graduated.

Most of the other girls were already pregnant or a mother by the time they reached sixteen.

Skamp's mother had moved away and left her with an uncle to raise her. But he was killed in a drug deal when she was only thirteen. Skamp then moved in with her boyfriend, who got her addicted to drugs and used her to sell them.

For many drug addicts, the cheapest and best way to afford drugs was to sell them. They weren't bad people, these drug dealers, just victims of their circumstances.

When Skamp's boyfriend died of an overdose, Skamp was once again out on the streets. For the past two years, she had survived by trading her body for drugs and sleeping in alleys and under parked cars.

She loved Carmen deeply.

Carmen was her only friend, the only one who hadn't turned her back on her. The two girls met secretly every night, and Carmen brought her food.

Sometimes Skamp was so sick that Carmen would sneak her into the apartment late at night for a hot bath and a clean change of clothes.

Carmen would sneak downstairs and wash and dry Skamp's clothes while her cousin took a nice hot bath.

Both suspected that Carmen's mom knew, but they never asked. Secrecy was the key to survival.

Carmen was a good girl, loved and respected by many throughout the project. She was not into drugs, sex, or trouble, like the other girls. Brave and daring, she seemed to want more out of life.

Several times, she had boyfriends secretly. Each time, Eddie would find out, beat up the boy, and end the relationship.

Carmen both hated and liked her big brother's protectiveness.

She knew that no one in the neighborhood would ever bother her or hurt her and that so many liked and respected her.

Sometimes, though, she secretly wished she could be as free as the other girls to have boyfriends and do things that were wrong. She knew that if she ever did *anything* wrong with someone else, no matter what, the other person would be punished.

Therefore, not wanting to get others in trouble, she always behaved—except with Skamp.

One day the gang decided to get pizza. Frankie, Eddie, and I started over to Pop's, a local pizza joint. We ran into Carmen and some of her friends.

"Carmen, you like my friend Jim, don't you?" Eddie grinned.

Carmen looked at me, her beautiful deep brown eyes penetrating mine; it was as if she could pierce my very heart. I felt uneasy.

Oh God ...please protect me ...she really gets to me. I don't want to cause problems for everyone ...but boy she makes my heart beat faster than it's ever beat before.

She smiled shyly at me and then nodded to Eddie. "Jim sure looks a whole lot better than any of you monkeys."

Everybody broke into laughter.

"Who you calling a monkey, you she ape?" Frankie bellowed.

"Yeah, my sister looks like a movie star compared to you," Eddie boasted.

I just tried to look into her eyes without being caught. Feeling my heart beating out of control, I decided to change the conversation. "Hey, let's get some pizza—Frankie's buying."

"Your mother's buying."

"Aw, Frankie," I said, "you know my mom's too cheap to buy a bunch of Puerto Rican hoods a pizza."

Leaning close, Frankie whispered in my ear, "Be careful, Jim. I see the way you look at Carmen and the way she looks at you. Our families are very firm about who they let their daughters date. You could get yourself killed." Frankie gave me a stern look and then winked.

He was right.

I had to learn to control my feelings and at the same time take the teasing they said about Carmen and me.

"Hey, Carmen," Frankie said in a soft voice, "why don't you and your other ugly friends join us for some pizza?"

Carmen smiled and extended a friendly finger to Frankie, then walked off.

We walked slowly to Pop's to get some pizza and sodas. It was the only restaurant in the project. Actually, it was more like a glorified deli.

Pop, being Italian, didn't like Puerto Ricans at all. He wasn't especially happy to have this group coming into his place, but money was money.

There were always about fifteen to twenty Italians shooting pool in the back room. The Italian gang, called the Knights, did not get along with the Puerto Ricans. Each had their own territory, but they allowed us to come into Pop's because they made money off us.

Sometimes things would get tense and everybody had to watch out. At a moment's notice, an explosion could occur. Though no one was stupid enough to carry (bring a gun), a drive-by shooting could occur later that night.

Among the Knights at Pop's that day was Tommy Scioto, the leader of their gang.

Frankie sneered at the girl with Tommy. "Would you look at those silly pants she's wearing?" he said, looking at Tommy's girlfriend. Frankie spoke loud enough for Tommy to hear.

Pop asked, "What do you punks want today?"

"Pizza, old man."

"Got any money?"

"Got anything that hasn't been spit on, old man? Give us two large pizzas, one pepperoni and one sausage. And hurry it up, Wop."

Name-calling was a delicate issue. Ethnic slurs in general were okay, but if used in anger or in a derogatory way, you could get hurt.

Frankie ambled over to the jukebox and picked out some songs.

"Hey, Tommy," one of his boys called out. "Geez, would you look at this, a Puerto Rican who thinks he can read."

"Nah, he knows only white guys can read; he's got all the buttons memorized."

Frankie ignored them and took his time selecting three songs.

Eddie called out, "Whadya pick out?"

"Just some classy love songs that make me feel romantic. And with all these pretty Italian girls here, I thought maybe I just might get me some lovin'."

"Fat chance of that, Puerto Rican, you don't even know the difference between a woman and a cow." Tommy sneered

Without looking up, Frankie said, "Oh, that's easy, these are classy looking women, and your momma is a cow."

Tommy just glared.

Pop called out, "Pizza's ready—if you have the cash."

"Don't worry 'bout it, old man; we lovers always got plenty of *dinero*, right Eddie?"

"Yeah, we get it from thankful young Wop girls."

Everyone picked up their pizza and a dozen beers and headed back to the projects.

We had walked about a block when a car filled with Italians sped by. It slowed, and the Italians pointed their fingers like guns and said, "Pow."

Sitting on the park bench in front of building fourteen, the gang ate the pizza and washed it down with the beer. Frankie began tapping an empty beer can with his pencil, and several guys started singing. Frankie stood and beat on the back of the bench like a drum.

Soon we had a whole band made of empty cans and bottles and a bench.

Jesus, I love these guys. They're real people, not like some of the phonies I knew back in college. These guys let me see who they really are. Please don't let me fail them.

It was after midnight when I returned to the three-story slum house that was my home. Immediately, I recognized the stink of fresh poop. Someone had pooped just inside the door, and I had to step over it to get to my apartment.

As I started down the hallway, I sensed that I was not alone.

"Got fifty cents, Mister?" a voice behind me whispered.

My heart skipped a beat. It was late at night, and everyone was asleep. If this was trouble, I was on my own.

Just ignore him and keep on walking; don't start a confrontation.

I continued toward my apartment. Only a few feet and I'd be safe.

"I'm talking to you, whitey. Answer me or die."

Just then, my apartment door flew open, and out stepped my roommate John-John. He was tall, muscular, and one mean man; he looked fearsome with his dark, unwashed, matted dreadlocks and cold, black eyes. Everyone who knew him stayed out of his way. I was sure glad that he was my roommate. John-John just stared at the intruder, who melted away.

I passed into the apartment with John-John behind, both of us saying nothing. I went to bed and pulled up the cover. I had learned a long time ago to sleep dressed, or some of my clothes might be missing in the morning.

Early the next morning I sat next to Caesar, who had a large cup of coffee in his hand. Staff meetings were held at 9:00 a.m., three times a week in Joey's apartment. Everyone working with Young Life was present. Clarkie and Gee took turns leading the Bible study. We prayed for each other, the kids we worked with, and everything going on in the neighborhood.

Next, Joey reminded us of the importance of our work. This was a dark and sometimes ugly neighborhood, and Young Life offered light and life to these oppressed youths.

"It's not always easy to love these kids," Joey said. This was followed by a loud uproar of laughter.

"You got that right," several said together.

Still, I knew I could do it, with Joey's guidance. He was one of the most caring, understanding, and courageous leaders I had ever met. He was teaching me to love not just in word but also from the heart.

Others recognized Joey's leadership as well. Some of the churches in the area got together to ask Joey to develop a program to help rid their neighborhoods of gang violence and drugs. In exchange, they paid the rent on the three apartments Young Life used and provided us with dinner each night.

Joey approached me following the staff meeting. "We need to talk. There's a jobs program coming soon. Each youth worker will get jobs for himself and all of his boys. You will get one hundred dollars a week, and each of your boys will make seventy."

I liked it so far. I had been working two part-time jobs emptying trashcans and clipping magazine articles at *Guideposts* magazine. Occasionally I got work through a local day labor company.

Joey went on. "Now here's the catch: all your work has to be done at the Douglas Elementary School. You are to keep the boys busy from nine to five. You think you can handle that?"

Joey was a good strong leader loved by everyone in the neighborhood and respected by all the gangs. His word was his bond. If he said he would do something, you could count on it.

"When does it start?"

"Next Monday. Now don't screw it up. Don't let anyone get into trouble, and make sure that everyone shows up for work each day and on time. Got it?"

"Sounds good to me."

"Who do we report to and what do we do?"

"Report to the janitor at nine o'clock sharp!"

I was excited. No more stinking day labor. No more waiting at some corner at 6:00 a.m. to compete with all the winos for some lousy job like cleaning up trash for a crummy twenty dollars that would be gone in a week. If I was lucky, sometimes it lasted two weeks.

Wow, one hundred dollars a week. If I worked for ten weeks, that money would last me for months.

I couldn't wait to tell Eddie and the others. Frankie could really use the money too.

They would all have a lot of fun and earn some great money—as long as I didn't screw it up.

Well, that's not going to happen, I promised myself.

"There is a way in a man's mind that seems right to him but the end of which is destruction." Joey stood before fifty young people gathered in the basement of St. Chris's Episcopal Church. It was Monday night, and that meant Young Life club meeting.

"Each person makes his or her own decisions. Therefore, each chooses his or her own destiny. But because disobedience is addictive, one little pleasure enjoyed—one little pleasure that we know to be wrong—can lead to an addiction of disobedience.

"I and I alone decide who I am going to follow. Everybody follows somebody or something. We all think that we are original, that we are free. But are we?

"Freedom is a choice—but you also can *choose* to be a slave."

"Why would anyone deliberately choose to be a slave?" someone in the crowd called out.

"Okay, I admit it sounds strange. What happens if I choose a life of drugs or sex or violence? Won't I eventually become a slave to it? When we realize that we are enslaved and trapped by our behavior, we sometimes cry out, 'Help me, God. I can't help myself.'"

Walking over to the small window and pointing outside, Joey continued. "Everybody out there makes choices every day. If I become a slave to God, then once again, 'I can't help myself' becomes my cry, but it is a cry of victory—of realizing that our true life and joy is found in being a slave to Jesus. Everybody follows something. Why not choose Jesus?"

Walking rapidly from one side of the room to the other, Joey raised his voice to an excited pitch. "As Christians we are happy *because* we are enjoying life more. We walk with a clearer conscience. We feel good about ourselves.

"And just like any addiction, it happens slowly over time. The more time we spend in our addiction, the more we become conformed to its lifestyle. Consequently, the more time I spend in God's Word, the Bible, getting to know Him better, and the more time I spend with my fellow Christians learning how to live a life pleasing to God, the happier I feel."

Stopping in the center aisle, Joey swept his hand around the room. "We all have the freedom to choose. In the Bible, Joshua says, 'Choose this day who you will follow …as for me and my family, we choose to follow the Lord.' The Bible also says that there are two roads we can choose to follow: one leads to life and happiness and the other to destruction."

Joey paused and looked around to let his words sink in.

"Isn't it great that we get to choose which master we will follow? If we want to take martial arts, we must decide which kind, which school, and what teacher we are going to call *Sensei* or Master."

Leaning back on the wall, Joey smiled his famous big grin.

"Every day we are forced—yes, forced—to make decisions, some small, some big. Some will affect our lifestyle. Sometimes our lifestyle is made up of all those small decisions. Sometimes our destiny is made up of the bigger decisions.

"If, for example, I make the decision to rob a small store to get some money to support my habit, and in the process, the store owner pulls out a gun and shoots me in the back, paralyzing me for the rest of my life, I can't be angry about that, because it was my decision—right? And I pay the consequences—right?"

A deep hush fell over the crowd as Joey's words sank in. They made perfect sense. Even those who had been whispering to one another paused to feel the impact. Some even looked a little scared.

Joey looked directly at a group of girls sitting against the wall and walked toward them.

"If you as a girl want children someday, but you decide that being liked is so important that you will have sex with anyone, and that leads to you getting a disease that prevents you from ever having babies—then *you* are paying for your decision. You can hate the guy who gave you the disease all you want, but it was your decision to say yes.

"If, on the other hand, you wait 'til marriage, and you have a wonderful marriage and healthy children, then it was a good decision."

Joey paused and smiled at the girls to show that he wasn't saying this in anger or judgment. Everyone knew that Joey had a really big heart and loved everyone equally. "Just don't let some guy ruin your life is all I am saying."

He walked over to a nearby wall and leaned his back against it. "Decisions are based on what you and I want. Saying yes to Jesus and following His commands can actually lead to a lifetime of freedom and happiness."

Joey held up his Bible for all to see. "In the Bible, there is a story of Jesus meeting a woman who had five husbands. She was so surprised that this stranger did not reject her even though He knew all about her; instead, He offered her forgiveness and love.

"So often we say, 'If ever you knew the real me, you would reject me'—right? Well the truth is that Jesus does know the real you and wants to forgive and love you too. Tonight you have the chance to accept His love and forgiveness. Or you can tell me to stuff it.

"Once again, the decision is yours. Think about it. We are going to close in prayer, and if you want to talk to me or Jim or any of the other staff, feel free to do so."

CHAPTER 5

O ne day Joey said, "Jim, you've been working some tough long hours with these guys. I was thinking why not take a couple of days and visit your friends in Washington, DC."

Wow, yes. Boy, was I excited. It had been almost a year since I had seen my friends. This was going to be great.

I arrived in Washington, DC, at about 4:00 p.m. Phil was waiting at the train station to pick me up. I talked excitedly as we rode. I was thrilled to be back among friendly friends, ones I didn't have to watch lest they steal my clothes. I couldn't wait to take a shower standing in a real bathtub.

"Jim, what's the first thing you want to do?"

"Ah, Phil, that's an easy one. I want some of Peggy's home cooking."

We both laughed. Phil had no idea that some days I went without something to eat.

As we drove the tree-lined streets with cars parked on both sides without broken windows or without being jacked up on milk crates with the tires stolen, I began to relax. This really was home. I couldn't wait to sleep in a real bed with fresh sheets. We had no sheets where I lived in New York.

Peggy met us at the door. After giving me a big squeezing hug, she said, "There are fresh towels on your bed." Turning her attention to Phil, she said, "Honey, how is he?"

"He'll be alright once he has a good meal and gets to see his friends."

Phil had invited the whole gang over. Many of them were home from college on vacation.

It was good to see Tuck, and Denise, and Fred "Rev" Harrison. This should have been a time of rejoicing, but that wasn't what was going to happen.

"So, Jim," Phil said, "how is it going? Joey says you are doing fine and that you are working with some pretty bad dudes. Ever get scared?"

"Does water run downhill?" I laughed. "Yeah, sometimes it can get pretty scary."

Tuck leaned forward to catch every word. "What's one of the scariest things that have happened to you?"

Looking around, and then speaking very softly, I said, "I haven't told anyone about this. It's kinda embarrassing. One afternoon I was coming back from the projects when I encountered a small crowd. There was a lot of noise going on. Working my way to the center of the crowd, I saw a man chasing an older man around a car. The younger man had a large knife. 'Please don't kill me,' the older man cried out. People were laughing. I couldn't believe they could be so cruel." I shifted in my seat. "I stepped forward and asked the young man to leave him alone."

"What happened?" Denise asked.

"He turned toward me, and he had a menacing look in his eye. If looks could kill, I would have been dead at that moment. 'You want some of me, whitey?' he taunted. Then he came running right at me swinging his knife, trying to cut me. I was so scared. I turned to run as fast as I could. Problem was I ran smack into a truck blocking my way."

"What happened then?"

"I froze! I couldn't believe it. After all my hand-to-hand combat training in the army, I froze. He walked slowly up to me. He looked like a crazed killer. Pointing his knife directly at the center of my throat, he touched the point of his blade against my chest and laughed. They all laughed. He turned and walked away, back to his group. I had on khaki pants, and I could feel a warm liquid running down my leg. There was a puddle by my feet. I was so embarrassed. Now I had to walk the rest of the way home with pee-stained pants."

"You didn't tell anyone?"

"No!"

Phil asked, "Wow—does Joey know?"

"Nope, I was too embarrassed. Please don't tell anyone, especially not Joey."

Denise smiled. "Well, that calls for a prayer of thanksgiving."

Everyone stood and formed a circle around me and thanked God for my deliverance. Soon the party broke up, and I went to bed early. I had a long day planned for tomorrow.

The next day I went to see Dr. Halverson, the pastor of Fourth Presbyterian Church, and my friend.

"Jim, come on in," Dick exclaimed warmly as he stepped around his massive desk to greet me.

It was always a pleasure to be in his presence.

"So, my friend, how is it going?"

"Right now, Dick, I just want to relax with my friends."

"Phil called me and told me that you were on your way and that it has been a rough year for you; is that so?'

"Yeah, New York is like a different country. Where I live is like a third-world country. People are so poor, there are no jobs, most people are on welfare, and the girls have babies just for the income the government pays them. The violence is so real and deadly. I sometimes wonder if I did the right thing going up there."

"I hear you, Jim; it is a rough and almost lawless place. I have a friend who is a pastor of a small church not far from where you live. He doesn't let his children go out to play. It's so sad."

He paused a moment and then changed the subject. "I hope you can stay for church."

"You kidding, I wouldn't miss it for the world. I came all the way down here just to hear you sing 'Great Is Thy Faithfulness'." Pastor Dick closed every evening service with that song.

After church, Phil took me to the train station.

"Good-bye, Jim, and may God always be your source of comfort."

The train ride was long, and I was sad. I was leaving safety and my friends again. Was I crazy?

"**Pissed your pants**!" Joey started laughing.

I was horrified. No one was supposed to tell Joey.

I hadn't even set my luggage down or gone to my room. He was standing in his doorway.

I must have turned six shades of red. "Yeah."

CHAPTER 6

Ricky cried out, *"Eddie, please, I was only kidding. For God's sake Eddie, I'd never challenge your authority as leader."*

"Thought you'd make a fool of *me*?" Eddie rose on his toes and leaned in so that his nose almost touched Ricky's.

"**A fool out of—me?**" Eddie's angry eyes told Ricky there was no use trying to explain. Eddie was furious; he would show no mercy.

Everyone was silent. The only sound cutting through the night air was the sickening *swooshing* sound of the short length of hose that Eddie swung at Ricky; it had been filled with sand and capped on both ends.

"**Son of a b…**" Ricky's anguished cry leaped from his lips followed by the snapping of leg bones as Eddie whipped Ricky again and again.

The hose was a favorite weapon because it crushed bones without breaking the skin. Thus, no messy bruises or blood.

Screaming in pain, Ricky crumpled into a heap on the ground. His shattered legs gave way, but his arms were held tightly by Teddy and Josh, two of Eddie's gang members.

"Didn't I tell you to stay away from Pop's? Didn't I tell you I would handle it? Just who did you think you are—going in there and starting a fight? I ought to kill you."

Eddie looked directly at Teddy and Josh. "Whadda ya think guys—should I kill him?"

Teddy shrugged his shoulders. "It's up to you. You wanna do it? Do it."

Eddie leaned over Ricky and spit in his face. Then, he kicked Ricky in the chest—hard. The *crack* of breaking ribs shattered the silence followed by more tormented crying

Teddy and Josh let go of Ricky, who slumped into a sobbing ball. Josh spat on him.

Eddie leaned close and whispered into Ricky's ear. "You better be gone, you and your family, by noon tomorrow, or I'll beat your mother to a pulp, and I'll let the boys have your scabby sister."

That was the punishment for challenging Eddie's leadership.

Hearing the loud screams as I approached the corner, I hastened my pace. Was Eddie in some sort of trouble? I could see Eddie and a couple of his boys standing in a circle. By the time I reached the spot, Eddie and the others had left. I found Ricky lying crumpled in a ball, bleeding and crying.

"Ricky, what happened?" I bent down to him.

"Get away from me," Ricky shouted. "Your buddy Eddie did this to me. I'll get even with the SOB if it's the last thing I do."

I backed away. I was in shock. I couldn't believe what I had just heard and seen. Eddie? Eddie did this? Why? What should I do? Shaking my head slowly, I walked back to my apartment.

The next day, Eddie and several of his friends were talking when I walked up.

"What's up guys?" I asked hesitantly.

Eddie and his friends looked at each other; then Eddie laughed. "The punk Ricky spoke to the Italians and gave them a message; said it was from me." They all looked at one another and laughed again.

"What happened? Why did he talk to the Italians?"

"Said they beat him up, and then Ricky told them that I would get their sisters. Punk spoke for me. But I fixed him last night."

Eddie snickered. "You won't see that sorry sucker around no more. Beat him bad last night." Eddie waved his hands in victory. "Really should have just killed him and dumped his body in front of Pop's restaurant."

Shocked, I just stood there. I had heard that Eddie had a bad temper and could really hurt people, but I'd never seen behavior like this. But, I also knew that Eddie would not kid me about something so serious.

How should I react?

Should I question Eddie's behavior in front of his friends?

No way!

But if I didn't do or say anything, then I as a Christian leader was condoning Eddie's brutality. What should I do?

I'd ask Joey later. Joey would know what to do; he always did.

Still, it troubled me. How could Eddie have such a loving and fun-loving side to him and be so brutal at the same time?

Eddie watched me as if waiting for a response.

What should I say?

I chose to ignore the issue. "I'm really hungry. You guys eaten breakfast yet?"

"Come on, chump." Eddie put his massive arm around my shoulder. "Let's go steal some food and eat." Everyone laughed.

Together we walked away from the others.

"So, what's up for today, Jim? I heard you had some important information for me."

I was confused. How could I just transition from that awful beating to the wonderful news of the new jobs?

Oh, God, help me. You said you'd give me wisdom when I needed it; well, I need it now.

I decided to let Joey handle it. "The city is sponsoring a work program for us to receive some job training and make money at the same time."

"What are you talking about?" Eddie asked. "The city don't do nothing for us; what's the catch?"

"No catch that I know of so far. I think the Feds are giving the cities money to help keep the crime rate down during the summer."

"You mean they're going to pay us, sort of a bribe, or protection money, to leave their precious city alone for the summer?"

"Appears that way."

"Man, you gotta be putting me on." Eddie smiled. "They're that afraid of us. Good—'bout time." He flexed his big muscles and spun around in a circle. "So how does it work?" Puffing out his chest, he strutted like a champion.

"All I know is that they'll pay you and twenty of your boys to work at one of the local schools."

"Doing what and how much?"

"Don't know what yet, but how's three hundred a month sound to you?"

"Three hundred? Wow! Definitely sounds good to me. When do we start?"

"Next Monday!"

"Wow, three hundred a month, for how long?"

"Joey says for the next ten weeks."

"Ten weeks, wow, that's seven hundred and fifty dollars. Do you know how much drugs your boy Frankie could buy for that?"

"Well, if he were still using at, say, twenty a day, that would be about thirty-seven days. Speaking of which, I'd like Frankie to be one of the workers. It'll keep him out of trouble."

"Well, he's your boy, and you're my man, so what can I say? Deal."

With Eddie looking extremely pleased, I walked along in silence. I definitely was not happy about what he had done to Ricky, though. I liked Ricky, just as I liked all the others.

And another thing: if Eddie would beat one of his boys so badly, what would he do if I ever pissed him off?

Joey shook his head. "It's a tough world out there, Jim. I'm sorry that you had to see this for yourself. Eddie's been known to really hurt some people badly, just on the spur of the moment; sometimes for no apparent reason at all—just for kicks. Eddie's a bad one—a real psycho— loves to hurt people when he gets the chance. Even his closest friends, if you can call them that, are afraid of upsetting him. People who know him steer clear when he's upset."

"I've heard some bad things about Eddie," I interjected, "but until today, I just didn't really believe them."

"Now here's the strange part. When he's in a good mood, he's like a little child; a lot of fun to be around." Joey shrugged his shoulders. "Just can't figure him out."

Joey sat back in his chair and closed his eyes.

"What now, Joey?"

"For these guys, it's a real jungle out there—survival of the fittest. That's why it's so important we reach them for Jesus."

"Do you think I can really make any difference with him?" I asked thoughtfully.

"Hang in there Jim; you're doing a good job. Eddie trusts you, and that's important. He's never allowed anyone to get this close to him before. God is using you in a mighty way with him. We can't reach them until we earn their trust."

Rising from his chair, he added, "I'm going to walk the neighborhood and talk to everyone so I know what's going on. Just remember, Jim, we, the team, are always here for you. Every day we pray for you and what God is doing through you."

I awoke the next day with a good feeling and a song in my heart.

Oh Jesus, I just know today is going to be a better day.

I sat down, opened my Bible, and studied for an hour.

Then I prayed for each of the guys and girls I worked with.

When I came to Carmen, I always struggled. What to pray for? Pray that I might get to know her better? That could be real trouble. Pray that she would somehow be able to escape this jungle?

The one thing I continually did pray for was that she would come to know Jesus and experience His freedom.

I finished getting dressed and went to the Corner Deli for breakfast. I had the same thing every morning around ten: two eggs over easy, toast, and chocolate milk. I usually read the front page of the newspaper while eating.

Sometimes, if I had an extra fifty cents, I would get a slice of chocolate cake. *Man, just think—one hundred dollars a week for the next eight weeks.* Wow! I was rich.

"You know that I don't like those guys," Scott said when he stopped by my table to chat. "But I got a lot of respect for you. If you ever need anything—anytime—call me—y' hear?"

"Thanks, Scott. I appreciate that *and* the good food."

By noon, I arrived at the projects. It was a ten-block walk from the deli, but I enjoyed it. Looking in the window of the bakery as I passed by, I reminded myself that soon I would have enough money to buy some donuts.

I felt excitement in the air as I headed to meet the guys. My job was simple, and I loved it: building relationships with these guys, helping them to get a job or into night school, giving them a chance to dream again, and enabling them to have a shot at achieving that dream.

But the most important thing for me was that I got to share the love and forgiveness of my Lord and Master, Jesus Christ.

CHAPTER 7

Every month, somebody died somewhere in the neighborhood. Some died of drug overdoses, some of gunshot wounds, and some from stabbings and beatings. No one was safe, especially the women. I believed that just maybe if I could help some of the guys to become good men with high standards, they would treat their women with respect.

One day I was sitting listening to Frankie tell about his problems with his girlfriend.

"Jim, I don't know what to do. My girl, she's really upset with me now."

"Tell me about it."

"Maria's been bugging me about having kids, but it's just so she can collect some welfare money."

"Still not planning on marrying her?"

"Why would I marry her?"

"Why not?"

"Man, why buy the cow when the milk is free? Besides, I don't know if I'm ready for that kinda commitment. I don't even know who my old man is. I don't know how to be a husband or a father. I don't know how to treat a wife."

"What about loving her and treating her right and making sure you take good care of her like the Bible says?"

"I love her, but not that kind of love. Man, what would happen if I treated her like gold and she betrayed me? Then I'd be the laughing fool, and I'd have to beat her right in front of everyone."

"Well, I know if it were me, I'd never want to lose her love, so I'd treat her like gold all the time."

"I've seen how you been looking at Carmen and the way she looks at you. Better stay away Jim; she's real trouble. Eddie would kill you if he found out."

"Sometimes it worries me too," I said rising from my chair. "Yeah, sometimes…." I laughed. "…Sometimes I get real scared. Let's go and get something to eat. I'll even pay for it."

"Thanks, you're all heart. I'm going to miss you when you're gone."

"Gone? Where am I going?"

"Well, you know, Joey has a lot of guys who come and stay for a while, but then they all leave."

"Where would I go? You guys have the best food and the best-looking women. Let's go and get something to eat."

Sitting at the lunch counter with Frankie, I asked, "Are you happy? I mean, really happy?"

"Why?"

"Frankie, what if you could break your habit and get out of the projects; where would you like to go, and what would you like to do?"

He thought carefully for a while. "I dunno. No one's ever asked me anything like that before. Y' know what I mean? I mean, everybody just lives and dies here. Nobody ever escapes."

"But what if you could? What if you were the first? What if you could be or do anything you wanted?"

Joey and Eddie were sitting on a bench in front of one of the apartments.

"I heard about Ricky," Joey said. "What happened?"

"Oh, that lame punk...." Eddie laughed. "Should have killed him—slowly, of course; would have been fun. But then I'd have to worry about somebody finding out, and I'd have to kill them too." He laughed again.

"Why do you like hurting people?"

"Why not? Your God hurt people he didn't like—right?"

"Maybe, but that was a long time ago, and you're not God."

"Says who? And you'd better be careful how you answer, Joey. To a lot of people, I *am* God."

A long moment of silence passed.

"I decide who lives and who dies here...me!"

"I hear what you're saying, Eddie. You think you're pretty tough, right?"

Eddie sat up straight and looked fiercely at Joey. "Got that straight—you saying I'm not?"

"No, what I'm saying is that I know that you're bad, but are you happy?"

"What's there to be happy about, living here?" Eddie waved his arms in a circle. "Someday somebody will kill me, or the police will take me away. Then someone else will take my place—maybe somebody meaner than me." Eddie puffed out his chest and glared at Joey. "One thing's for sure, I ain't ever getting out of here except maybe in a body bag."

"It doesn't have to end that way, you know."

"Yes it does. Who's gonna help me—your Jesus?"

"Could be, but that'd be up to you. You'd have to make some changes in your life."

"Too late for me, Joey; I seen too much, done too much. God doesn't want somebody like me."

"Well, Eddie, maybe and maybe not." Joey measured his words carefully. "There have been a lot of guys just like you who have done some wrong things in their lives, and still God accepted them into His family—forgave them and all."

Eddie took a long drag on his cigarette, inhaled the smoke, and then blew it out slowly making smoke rings. Then he got up and walked away.

Joey sat and prayed silently for Eddie. He was one bad dude, but there was room in God's heart for him. Joey just wasn't sure how to reach him.

Joey got up and started after Eddie. There was something important he needed to tell him, and quickly.

Eddie walked up to the corner and stopped. He looked around at the neighborhood. *Yeah, someday I'll die here, but I'll take a lot of them with me.* He stomped out his cigarette and kept walking.

Popping open a bag of hard candy, Frankie carefully unwrapped a piece. "What would I like to be if I ever got out of here?"

He shifted in his bunk bed and looked directly at me.

"Maybe a welder. Yeah, that's it, a welder."

"A welder?"

"I got a cousin, Vinny, in Chicago; he's a welder. I met him at my aunt's funeral. He says he's got this big place on the West Side and has a brand new car and one for his wife. Wears nice clothes, too. Me, I never been out of the neighborhood; can you believe that?"

Standing up and walking around in a circle, Frankie continued. "I live in New York City, the capital of the world, and I've never even seen Broadway or Rockefeller Square or nuttin'."

"Do you know how to get in touch with your cousin in Chicago?"

"My mom does."

"Well, tomorrow we'll talk to your mom and tell her you kicked your habit and that you'd like to get in touch with your cousin."

"That'll work. Y'know, when you first came here, I thought you were just like all of the other guys before you. Most of them only lasted a couple of weeks. There was this one guy, his name was Tony—man, we gave him such a hard time, he split without even saying goodbye." Frankie laughed so hard he fell into the wall.

"What did you do?"

"We set him up with this junkie hooker named Tina. One night when he went to bed after we were sure he was asleep, we sent Tina in, and she took off all her clothes and slipped in bed with him. Then we pounded on the door and went in and turned on the lights as he woke up. He bolted upright. There he sat, naked as a jaybird, with Tina alongside him, rubbing her arms and saying he was too rough on her.

"We screamed, '**Tony, what in the world are you doing with Tina? That whore has AIDS! If you wanted to get laid, we could have fixed you up with a real woman.**'

"Tony came wide awake and saw all of us and Tina, jumping up he rushed naked to the bathroom and threw up. In the morning, he packed up and left. We never saw him again."

Frankie was laughing so hard that spit dribbled from his mouth. These guys lived and played hard and fast. They had no time for phonies or do-gooders.

I believed that Jesus had paid a big price for me and that I was just as bad a person as these guys were, so I kind of felt a kinship with them. I had never really done anything truly bad, but I had thought about it many times.

I often had dreams about making wild, passionate love to Carmen. Was it because I really loved her? There was something so special about her, and it was so hard to know the difference between lust and love. One thing was for sure, I didn't know if I would ever have a chance to be alone with her and find out how she felt about me.

I felt that just under the skin we were all alike. The only difference was that I could pick up at any time and go home—wherever that was. One thing I knew; I couldn't go back to living in a small town now that I'd experienced the big city, so for me, there was no going back.

In reality, everyone is pretty much alike. We all have dreams, and we all have things that hold us back. Being victims of our own fears is how many of us live our entire lives.

Just then, Eddie came walking up. "So how's the two queens of the universe doing?"

Frankie replied, "I got your queen."

Eddie continued the nasty talk. "Aw, you wouldn't know a good woman if she sat on your lap." It was all good fun, because these guys had grown up together and known each other all their lives. They were family.

"Ya momma's so ugly, no wonder you turned out deformed," Frankie retorted

Frankie's remark stung not only Eddie but me too, because of my love for Carmen. But now was not the time to take up for her.

CHAPTER 8

"Hey...hey, wake up guys. We got a problem." Joey stood directly over me in the dark of the night. He hadn't even bothered to turn on the lights because he didn't want to wake the others.

"Get dressed quickly and meet me out front."

I jumped out of bed, grabbed my pants and shirt, and pulled them on quickly. After stopping to put on my sneakers, I ran down the hall.

Outside in the dark, I could barely make out the faces of the rest of the team. Clarkie and Gee were there, and Bo was quickly coming up the sidewalk. Caesar and Joey came out the door.

"Thanks guys; let's roll. Trouble is stirring in the project. A big fight is brewing between the gangs. We gotta stop them before the cops get there or someone gets killed. Otherwise, there'll be no peace for a while."

Man, what a way to wake up. Why can't these guys ever fight during the day? It always seems to be at night—in the middle of the night.

Caesar broke into my thoughts. "Jim, I'll see if I can get Eddie to calm down some of his boys; you talk to the rest."

"Right! I'll take the boys from Ronny's building."

When we arrived at the project, I was out of breath from running ten blocks.

The grounds were full of activity. Lots of guys were swarming around the few benches, as well as some girls, and everyone was shouting. Cars were parked along the curbs with engines racing and radios blaring Italian songs.

Leaders from the city's community youth outreach program along with Father Tomas from St, Chris's Episcopal Church and Father Ryan from the Chinese Lutheran Church met with all of us.

Joey and some of the city workers and the priests went over to the side and put their heads together. After about half an hour, they came back. "Tell everyone to go back to bed. Father Ryan and Father Tomas will handle it."

Whatever "it" was, that was good enough for me. Both priests were well respected.

Cesar and I talked to Eddie. "I don't know what went down, but the priests said they would handle it," I told Eddie. "What happened, anyway?"

Eddie laughed. "Some black guy talked to an old white woman, some stupid Pisano. She couldn't understand what he was asking and started screaming. All of a sudden, there were a bunch of those Pisano's running across the street looking for him—looking for someone to beat up. Big shots—took twenty or more of them to come looking for one black boy."

Turning and walking away, I said, "Well, I for one am glad to go back to bed and get some sleep."

Eddie puffed up his chest. "Not me. I'd rather shoot one or two of them just for the fun of it."

Someone shouted out from the crowd, *"Don't worry, Eddie, y'll get your chance to kill somebody soon—I can just feel it."*

"Eddie, wait up." Joey hastened his pace.

Eddie had already covered three blocks before Joey caught up with him. Eddie seemed in a hurry. He paused and turned around. "What's up?"

"I know that I told you about the new jobs starting tomorrow. It's important to me and to all of us that you make sure that none of your boys steals anything. It could get the whole program cancelled."

"So why you telling me? My boys don't steal unless I tell them to."

"Exactly my point. You know that someone stole the Seven Stations of the Cross from St. Chris's Church. Unless we get them back, Father Tom will not be able to let us use his church for our club meetings. I can't afford to have us kicked out of the church. Not only do they let us meet there, but they pay for my apartment—so it's personal now."

Eddie walked on in silence and then crossed the street. Joey went home.

The next day Father Tom called Joey. "Don't know what you did, but thanks. I found all the Stations of the Cross back in their original spots in the church. Again, thanks."

Joey smiled as he hung up the phone.

After this narrow escape, I looked forward to some peace and quiet. However, I was wrong.

CHAPTER 9

From the beginning, Caesar and Frankie, two of my roommates, had been my closest friends. They helped me adjust to life in the neighborhood. Frankie was a fun guy and I really liked him, but he was constantly getting high on heroin. Frankie would resort to stealing to pay for his drugs—he even stole from me—even though I couldn't prove it. One night he asked me to help him quit drugs by going "cold turkey." Cold turkey meant staying locked up in our room for three days and nights. He would not have any drugs, and I would help him detox his body. This meant feeding him lots of hard card to ward off his cravings for drugs, and finding a way to occupy both of us without going out.

I told Joey of our plans, and he asked me if I was aware of the cost to both Frankie and me. He told me that Frankie had tried this once before with another person, and in the midst of a painful crisis during those three days, Frankie had beaten the other guy unconscious.

When we met with Frankie to discuss it, Joey turned to him and said, "Do not hurt Jim! I am warning you, if you hurt him, I will hurt you—bad."

I was so excited about helping Frankie that I figured I could handle him.

Boy was I wrong! On the second day, Frankie, full of withdrawal pain, attacked me, and we both fought for our lives. I had never been in a real fight before, and this one was for real. He wanted out of the apartment, and I had locked the door and had the only key. A person on drugs is not in his or her right mind, and for some reason, Frankie seemed to be full of super strength. When he attacked me, there was no way I would be able to fight him off. I just had to trust him and hope that Joey was wrong.

Smash! Pain! Blinding light! I was sound asleep when Frankie attacked. Suddenly, I was in the fight of my life. He had me pinned against the wall of my lower bunk bed. I couldn't move, nor could I breathe. I felt helpless.

Gathering all my strength, I hit him hard in both ears at the same time and pulled my feet up under him and pushed him off. He flew through the air just far enough for me to get out of my bed. Then charging me like a bull and trying to drive me back into the bed, head down, he flew straight at me. I sidestepped him and stuck out my right foot so that he tripped and went sailing into my bed. His head smashed into the wall.

Immediately, I dove onto him, landing on his back. As he tried to get out of the bed, I kept pounding him on the back. Turning over rapidly, he came up suddenly and hit me hard, right in the middle of my face. The pain was incredible. There was a blinding flash of light, and I fell back against the wall.

Joey heard the racket and came flying up the stairs. He burst through the door and slammed Frankie against the wall. Shouting, "**Stop! Didn't I tell you not to hurt Jim?**"

He was mad at both of us, and he threatened Frankie not to touch me again. I took a shower, and Frankie and I both fell asleep.

The next morning I felt like a big truck had smashed into me. My nose hurt, my eye was swollen shut, and my entire body was wracked with pain. I sat on the edge of my bed and thanked God I was still alive. I didn't know it at the time, but Frankie was upstairs in Joey's office.

There was a knock on the door; opening it I was surprised to see it was Carmen's cousin Skamp.

"Jim come quick! Carmen wants to see you," she exclaimed.

If Carmen wanted to see me, that was very important.

"She's under the bridge—quickly!"

What could this mean? I threw on my pants and shirt and jumped up to follow her out.

If Eddie knew that I liked Carmen, or even if he found us together, we would both die. Running to the bridge as fast as I could, I found Carmen hiding in the shadows.

"Jim, oh thank God! You look terrible. I was afraid that Frankie would kill you. I love you so much and do not want to see you die." She looked like an angel. Her hair was pulled back into a ponytail, revealing more of her beautiful face. I was at once beholding the most beautiful woman God had ever made, and the woman of my dreams.

It was a dream come true—Carmen loved me. Wow! I wanted to shout it out to the whole world, but I knew I couldn't. I held her close, gently turning her head up to face me, her lips touching mine. We kissed, and *passion* burned through my whole body.

From around the corner, Frankie came running fast. "Get out of here," he shouted. "Eddie's on his way here." We kissed once more; a fire was blazing in both of us, and my mind was reeling. What would become of us? We said a quick goodbye and went our separate ways.

The next day as I walked back to my apartment, I ran into Joey. "Have you seen Frankie?" he asked.

"No."

"Well, just be warned. He's higher than a kite again."

"**What**?" I exploded. "What happened?"

"He hooked up with José, and Jose gave him some drugs."

"José? I told José to stay away from him. **I'll kill Jose**."

"**You'll do no such thing**. I warned you that this could happen. Just let it go."

Just let it go? Who was he kidding?

I raced back to the apartment, and there was Frankie grinning from ear to ear just as high on drugs as before we started. "**Frankie**," I shouted. "**How could you**?" He just grinned. He was so high, he was totally happy.

I flew out the door and went looking for José.

Hoping he was in the projects, I got on the bus that would take me to the projects and was just about to sit down when I saw José sitting in the rear of the bus.

"**José!**" I screamed loudly. "**I'm going to kill you**." Everyone on the bus was black, including José. They looked at me like I was crazy, not only for threatening one of their own, but everyone knew José was a drug dealer, and you didn't mess with any of Bennie's drug dealers.

Bennie was "Mr. Big" of the drug dealers. The average drug dealer was just another addict who needed to sell drugs in order to get some money to buy his own drugs. Drug dealers could not carry any weapons to defend themselves against robbers because if the police caught them with weapons on them, they would go to jail. So Benny ruled very viciously. Anyone who hurt or robbed any of his dealers would die a horrible death that same night, and their body would be dumped in plain sight for all to see. That was how Bennie protected his dealers.

As I raced down the aisle toward the back of the bus, the driver hit his brakes and came to a screeching halt throwing me off balance and into a seat occupied by a scared woman. She screamed, and I jumped up and resumed my chase for José.

The rear door flew open, and José plunged down the stairs and into the night. I leaped down the stairs, just seconds behind him. I reached for his long hair, but just missed. I pulled on the emergency cord. The bus driver quickly closed the door, started up again, and drove away. There was nothing I could do but sit down. I got off at the next stop and walked back home. I cried most of the way. I wasn't sure who I was crying for, but I just cried.

Walking away, I could hear some woman on the bus saying, "Bennie gonna get him. Nobody messes with José; he's one of Bennie's key players. Oh yes, when Bennie do get him and we all know Bennie will find him; yes, Bennie will get him, and it will be tonight. In the morning there he will be for all to see, badly beaten to death." I tried to shut her out, but I just couldn't.

I was so hurt! I wanted to find José and kill him before Bennie found me and killed me. At least I would die a hero to some.

Sitting in my apartment I tried to sort things out when I heard a loud knock at the door. At first, I ignored it, then it got louder, and a loud voice said, "**Open up, Jim.**"

No! I shouted in my mind. *I'm not ready to die yet. Maybe it's not him.*

I opened the door and my heart stopped.

There stood two very tall and very strong men who worked for Bennie. "Bennie wants to see you."

I walked outside with them. One man went to the passenger door of a big black limo and opened it for me to get in. As I entered, he gave me a slight shove. The other man walked around and got into the driver's seat. It was so dark I couldn't see. But I could smell Bennie from his cigar smoke. This was just like something you would see in a movie: a drug lord forcing me into the back seat of the car for a one-way ride to death. I was scared—very scared.

We rode quietly for several minutes. Finally Bennie spoke. "You know what you did was wrong, Jim. Now you know what I gotta do to you."

I was so scared I couldn't speak. I sat there terrified. When we reached a dark area near the waterfront, Bennie said, "Pull the car over here." Now I knew it was all over.

Oh Lord, it seems so unfair. Why did you bring me here? Why did you ever give me such a love for these kids?

Bennie leaned forward. He had on a long fur coat and a velvet hat with a feather in it. "Jim, you know that I have a duty to protect my men. They have to be able to trust me. You know that I have to kill you."

Just let me go and I'll disappear.

Bennie just sat there and stared deeply into my eyes.

"I'm going to let you live. You know why? Because I've watched you over the months, and no one has ever come here from the outside like you have and shown so much love for my people. You're an educated white man. You could go anywhere and make lots of money without having to risk your life here. So I'm going to give you a break this time, but if you ever...."

I quickly cut him off and said, "Never again, Bennie—never again." And I meant it.

CHAPTER 10

After waiting what seemed like a long, long time, the school job finally came through.

On the first day of work, Eddie and his boys showed up on time.

The first two weeks cleaning the school went fairly smoothly. We were now halfway through the third week.

Just then, Johnny came running up. "Eddie, we got trouble."

Eddie and I walked quickly into the school. Several of the guys were standing around in the hallway. "**Wasn't me, Eddie**! …wasn't our fault. I was throwing a bucket of dirty water out the window when the window fell down and the bucket went through it." Several of the guys snickered.

Just then, the janitor came running into the room. "What was that sound of glass breaking?" Spinning around he saw one of the windows broken.

He glared at Eddie and stuck his finger in Eddie's face. "I told you, Mr. Wise Guy, that you and your boys had better not break anything.

Well, this is gonna cost you. You're gonna pay for that window, one hundred dollars." The old man glared at Eddie.

"**That stupid window don't cost no hundred dollars. I'll get it fixed myself for ten**." Eddie leaned in close to the janitor and stared him in the face.

"Well, it don't work that way here in my school, Mr. Wise Guy. It's gonna cost you one hundred dollars."

"Don't push me, old man. I just might have to hurt you."

"**What, you threatening me, punk?**"

"Wait, calm down sir," I pleaded. "I'm sorry we broke your window. I'll get it fixed. We didn't mean to break it, and these kids need a job. Please don't take this way from them—please."

"**Just what do you think you're doing, Jim?**" Eddie bellowed. "**I don't need you to speak for me or my boys—stay out of it. And as for you, old man, get out of here—now!**"

The old man fled promising to call the cops.

Suddenly, I lost it. Months of pent-up rage, at always allowing Eddie to be right, especially when I knew Eddie was wrong, came to the surface. Months of his making a fool out of me, just so he would look cool. "**Eddie, stop!**" I hollered, with a defiant stare at him. "**You are about to cost us this whole job program. I can't afford to lose this program. Joey's counting on me—on us.**"

"**Screw Joey—screw you—and screw the city. We don't need this stinkin' job.**"

"**No, screw you, Eddie!**" I screamed so loud, I could swear I heard the windows rattling. My throat felt tight. I had never before spoken out to anyone like this. I was always so afraid to express my true feelings to anyone.

"You think that you are so big and bad; well, you just cost all of us our jobs, and our money. You just cost me money I really needed."

Anger welled up deep inside of me. Never had I spoken in such rage to anyone. I was so angry with Eddie, not just for killing the jobs program but for hurting Joey's larger program with the city, and for hurting any chances I had with Carmen.

Turning, I walked away and headed toward the door.

"**Where do you think you're going, punk**?" Eddie shouted after me, his voice rising in anger. "**Get your punk ass back here. You leave when I say you leave**."

"**Screw you**," I screamed as I walked away, reaching over my shoulder and extending him a finger.

Walking quickly to get away from such an angry confrontation, I suddenly began to cry. My emotions were running wild. *What had I just done? What would Joey say?* I tried to figure out just how to explain it to Joey. He was *not* going to be happy.

"You ok?"

I sat in Joey's office, my head laying off to one side, eyes closed. I'd been up since 6:00 a.m. Sleep had been a horrific experience. All night long, I tossed and turned with one nightmare after another.

"I don't know, Joey. Yesterday was a bad day"

"So I heard." Joey took a slow sip of his coffee.

"Ruined my new jobs program, didn't you?"

I sat there in silence and disgust. Tears were welling up, I had made a shambles of something Joey worked so hard to get for us. *Come on, Joey, say something nice.*

"Just kidding, Jim—you've done a great job. Things just got a little out of control. I heard Bennie came to visit you the other night. How'd that go?"

"He said that if I screwed up again, he'll kill me; said that I have to leave his boys alone."

"How do you feel about that?"

"Confused."

"Because…?"

"Because I need time to think. I mean, part of me believes these guys are worth saving, and part of me doesn't anymore."

"Tough place to be, Jim. They are worth saving, but there are no shortcuts. To save them, you gotta bear the pain—just like Jesus did for you."

"Pain—that's all I've known lately."

I'm tired of all the pain. I just want things to go really well for a change, even if it's only a couple of days."

"Know what you mean. I've been there myself. I got an idea. Why don't you take a week off and go uptown and visit Michael and his Mennonites. I will make a call and let him know that you're coming up. Just go and get some rest. Hang out with them for a while and have some fun."

The next morning, Joey and the rest of the team were deep into prayer praying for a peaceful solution.

"**Joey, Jim's in trouble**," Frankie said as he came bursting through the open door into Joey's apartment." **Eddie's really angry at Jim for embarrassing him in front of his boys. He's got a gun and he's drinking. Soon he'll be coming here looking to kill Jim**."

Rising up quickly, I stumbled and fell over the chair. *Now what? What do I do now? God, when is this all going to end?* I finally managed to stand straight and leaned against the wall. "**What? What did you say Frankie?**" Terror filled my entire being.

Sweat ran down my face, my knees went weak and wobbly, and I almost collapsed.

Joey came up to me and hugged me. "Sit down for a moment," he whispered into my ear. He gently guided me back to a chair, and I slowly sat down. My mind was a blank and my emotions were numb.

"Jim, I hope you knew that there was always the danger that working with these guys could end in your death, perhaps even a violent death. That's the chance we take when we work with people who don't know the Lord and whose lives are filled with fear and violence."

Joey paused and said to Frankie, "Get Jim a cup of coffee, please."

Taking a deep breath, Joey exhaled slowly. "Jim, I gotta ask you to think about something. I want you to think about this carefully. *Are you afraid to die?*

"Since the year 33 AD, Christians have faced death for following Jesus. You know that. Even today, Christians living in Muslim countries face death every day for their faith. Just for believing in Jesus, they suffer. They're beaten, tortured, and killed—sometimes horribly."

Leaning back in his chair, hands behind his head, Joey said, "You, on the other hand, have committed an act worthy of death. You defied and embarrassed a mighty powerful man in my community. I know that you love these guys—even Frankie knows that. But you went over the line. True, it was out of love when you defied Bennie on behalf of Frankie, but it was out of stupidity in Eddie's case."

I winced at that statement about Eddie. Joey was right. I should have let Joey handle it. It was stupidity on my part; more than that, it was arrogance. It was like I had said to Eddie, "I top dog; you dumb gang leader." What to do? Ok, so I did wrong—but still I didn't want to die. I had so much I wanted to live for.

True, I was fed up with my life at this point, but it could always be started over again somewhere else. Marriage, children, and grandchildren sounded like a lot of fun. I wanted to see if there was a future for Carmen and me. Helping Frankie get free, yeah, that really mattered to me. Dying now was not what I wanted.

Oh God, you promised that if I gave my life to you and followed your commands, that you would give me the desires of my heart. Well, right now my desire is not to die. I spent my life up here serving you—you owe it to me.

"Jim," Frankie said with urgency in his voice, "You gotta get out of here, now."

"Frankie's right," Joey echoed. "It's time for me to call Michael. Go up to his place for a few days and let me see if I can work something out with Eddie. In the meantime, relax; take a vacation. Go see a movie; take one of those pretty girls out on a date. And while you're up there—pray a lot about whether you should come back or just move on."

I sat there unable to move. I didn't know what to do. Sure, I wanted to live, but I was no coward. I wasn't gonna run away from Eddie.

"Come on, Jim, get up. Frankie, throw some of his clothes together into my trash bag. Here's twenty dollars. Now go!"

Still feeling numb, I got up. I didn't want to go, what if Joey couldn't work it out with Eddie, would I ever be able to come back? But I knew that these two guys loved me and that I wasn't thinking straight right now and possibly they were right.

Frankie came back with some of my clothes, took me by the arm, and led me out of the door and down to the closest subway stop, moving as quickly as he could. He put two tokens in the machine and pushed me through the turnstile. Once on the inside, Frankie guided me up the long concrete platform to where the train would stop and where the closest door most likely would be.

Soon the bright light of an approaching train could be seen and then whoosh the train came flying in. It slowed down quickly and came to a stop. All the doors opened at the same time. I still felt numb just standing there. Good thing Frankie had his senses about him.

"I love you, man," Frankie said as he pushed me into one of the train cars. "Take care—hope to see you again."

Yeah, me too.

I walked slowly to a seat and sat down. Looking up, it felt as if everyone in the subway car was looking at me and they knew! I tried to take my mind off things, but it didn't work. Sitting there would give me a lot of time to think.

What is this all about? What in the world has happened? One day everything is fine. In fact, it couldn't have been better. Carmen sent for me and told me she loved me. Wow! A smile crossed my lips—people probably wondered what I was thinking. *Some kiss! I had it made. Why did I get so upset with Eddie? I don't know—don't know much anymore.*

I heard a small quiet voice in the back of my mind.

"Jim, do you not know that I love you? I have always loved you."

I don't know. I am so confused! God, if that is you, please help me.

CHAPTER 11

The train slammed to a screeching halt and I stumbled as I got up from my seat. Funny, I had ridden these trains hundreds of times and yet I still forgot to hold on when it stopped. I made my way out of the car and up to another level and over to another set of tracks that would take me up to where Michael lived.

As I stood there, a menacing-looking man started walking toward me. *What now? Does he want to kill me too?* I stood there watching him approach. Slowly and carefully, he walked straight toward me.

"Gotta cigarette, man?" he asked.

I shook my head no and walked away from him. The man turned and walked back to where he had been.

Oh, God…Oh, God was all I could think—all that kept running through my mind.

"Jim, what's the emergency?" Michael's tone was urgent; my face was twisted with concern.

Looking up I saw Michael walking rapidly toward me. Joey had called him and asked him to meet me. Joey was kind enough to explain that this was an emergency and that I would explain it to him when I got there.

Michael looked like every mom's dream man for her daughter to marry. He was about five feet ten inches with dark black wavy hair, blue eyes, and a very handsome face, and he always had the warmest smile.

The walk from the subway stop to Michael's was long. "I'm in deep danger," I told him. "Someone is trying to kill me."

I had come all the way from the Lower East Side of Manhattan to 125th Street and Amsterdam, the heart of violent black gangs.

Feelings of shame and fear welled up in me. I did not want Michael to see my tears—no, I would not let him see them. He and I were leaders, strong Christian leaders, and leaders didn't cry. I had learned that much in my eighteen-month stay here. One thing men do not do is admit fault or cry. We'd rather go down fighting than admit that we were wrong.

Michael reached out and took the trash bag that I was carrying. In it were all my worldly possessions: some underwear, socks, and a change of clothes, along with my Bible and a pen.

We walked in silence 'til we reached his place.

Hiking up the two floors to Michael's apartment wore me out.

"Hungry?"

"Yeah, I guess so."

"Well, Dianna's a great cook. You've met Dianna, my wife, haven't you?"

Reaching past Michael, Dianna gave me a big squashing hug. "Of course he knows me, dummy." The look in her eyes was one of love and sadness. She knew I had come because there was a threat on my life. "Come on in, Jim, have a seat."

There were ten other youth workers already sitting at the table waiting to eat.

"Sit down, Jim, we're hungry," one of them called out with a laugh.

I sat down and thought I could not eat. I was so upset. Before I knew it, I had eaten two plates full of Dianna's great rice and beans. They weren't wealthy; in fact, most of them were volunteers, so meals were sparse. No one brought up the subject of why I was visiting.

I was glad. I just didn't want to talk about it. I needed time—time alone with God, and then some time with Michael. I valued his advice. Michael had been working in Harlem for several years.

He showed me to a guest room and then left me alone. He knew that I would talk to him when I was ready. I set my bag on the bed and sank down to my knees.

"Oh, God, what am I going to do? I don't wanna die," I cried out.

Tears were streaming down my face. My shoulders were shaking. Soon my whole body was trembling. Mucus came streaming out of my nose almost drowning me.

I began to sob. I felt numb. I prayed inwardly, not wanting anyone to hear my anguish.

Oh God, what am I gonna do?

If I go back, Eddie will kill me for sure.

Y'know, it's not that I am afraid of dying. It's just that I really haven't had a chance to live yet.

I want to know for myself what being loved is all about.

I stared at the ceiling.

Everyone says it's so wonderful. I would love to get married and have sex with Carmen. I want to have kids and have someone to play with.

*MOST OF ALL, I JUST WANT SOMEONE TO LOVE ME—
ME—JUST ME, not me the Christian youth worker, not me the
leader, but me—just me—with all my faults.*

Why did I have to be so foolish as to challenge Eddie? Now what?

Oh God, have I been wrong all along?

Is there really a God?

Do you really exist?

"Oh God, I hurt so much—please help me!" I whispered.

I crawled over to the bed, slowly pulled myself up, and flopped
onto it.

"Have I been a really stupid fool for giving up everything, every
pleasure of life, and the freedom to just be myself and do my own thing
if you don't really exist?"

I felt emboldened.

"**ANSWER ME**—I've earned the right to know!"

I paused and waited to see if God really would answer.

*Do you really not know me? I have known you all of your life. I know all
of your mistakes, all of your faults and sins, and still I love you.*

"Oh, God, it's just is so hard. Deep in my heart, I know you love
me, but sometimes it seems like I've been a really big fool. I mean come
on, look at me—what do you see? A white man twenty-four years of age
trying to live among people I don't even know and trying to tell them
that their way of living is all wrong and only my way is right. What do
I know?"

God didn't answer me. By this point, I was talking to myself anyway.
I had to get it out.

"How stupid can I be? Why did I ever think that because I am white
and a Christian, I am always right? Ok, so they are Puerto Rican and have
different rules, different values. Many of them say they are Christians,
but they smoke, drink, and really enjoy themselves. Is smoking wrong?
Drinking? They can't all be wrong—can they? Here I come along with

my conservative white Christian values and tell them that to be happy in Jesus they need to give up all the fun stuff and be miserable like me."

I thought about what I had just said. It just slipped out before I even had a chance to think: miserable. *Yeah, that's right*, I thought. *I am miserable.*

"Am I making any sense, God?"

I pounded my fist into my pillow. "**You make me so angry—are you even listening?**"

Suddenly, I was all played out. I had no more anger or strength left in me.

I just lay there and stared into space.

Are you finished?

I lay there quietly as a "voice" ran through my thoughts.

"Remember, Jim that I am abiding in you, just as your life abides in me. There is nothing you have thought or done that I do not know, and still I love you.

CHAPTER 12

Michael came and woke me. "Come on, Jim; we're getting ready to have some prayer. Afterwards I want you to tell us what this is all about."

Sitting in a circle, there were about six young Mennonites present. Four were girls and two were guys. All were in their early twenties, just like me. The girls were really pretty. One girl, Alecia, had eyes so blue and mischievous. There was a sparkle in her eyes as she smiled at me.

They all seemed like such good and decent Christians. Each had come here to the city to be a missionary for a two-year program their church sponsored. Once it was over, they were free to go home. Here in the city, it was such an ugly jungle, and these nice kids seemed to be out of their element.

Michael, the group leader, had been there two years already and was staying for one more year. Were any of them even aware of why I was there? What would they think of me when I told them? I had known

Michael for about a year, but I didn't know most of the others, especially any of the girls.

"Let's start by singing a couple of praise songs," Michael said. Soon everyone was singing and clapping and having a wonderful time. It reminded me of similar times back in college, long before I came here to the city. God, those days seemed so far away now.

Could I go back to my old life in DC? I had my doubts. I was a different person now.

I was torn. Could I stay here, or would my newfound doubts and skepticism cause problems with these young and seemingly naïve Mennonites from Lancaster, Pennsylvania?

All I knew was that I was a different person from when I arrived eighteen months ago.

The singing ended and everyone sat down. Michael read a passage from the 23rd Psalm: "The Lord is my Shepherd, I shall not fear. What do you think God meant when He said that?" asked Michael

There was total silence for a few minutes.

"Do you think that means that we shouldn't lock our car doors or the house at night?"

"Well," Jeremy, the youngest, said, "wouldn't that be foolish? Bad people live all around here, and they would just love to come in and steal from us while we are asleep, and what about the girls? Who would protect them?"

Michael shifted in his chair and looked me directly in the eye.

"Jim, the next part says that He will take care of us and protect us even when we walk through that fearsome valley of death. What do you think? What has been your experience?"

Before I could answer, Michael said to the group, "For those of you who don't know Jim, he's one of us, one of the good guys. He loves the Lord, and God called him to do something special for Him.

"Yes sir, ole Jim had it made back on the University of Maryland campus. He was a leader in a couple of Christian groups and had several Christian girls all wanting to be his girl.

"So there he was living this ideal life and loving it—you did love it, didn't you Jim?"

"Yeah," I said, snickering. "I did love it. I was somebody special, and I was loved by several girls. Biggest thing, though, was that I was the leader. No one tried to change me. Everybody just did as I asked."

Michal smiled and looked at me with warmth and compass. "Not quite like that up here in the city, is it Jim? Why Jim, I could just see you, brother, marching down there into that dark ghetto and demanding that they stop their cussing and drinking and give their lives to Jesus. You wouldn't be afraid of that would you?"

Michael stared directly at me as if waiting for an answer, and then he quoted another section from Psalm 23. "Yea though I walk through the valley of the shadow of death, I will fear no evil. Why is that?"

When I didn't have a ready answer, Michael asked, "Why would a brother fear no evil?"

"Cause he just ain't too bright," Tony said; he was the smartest and oldest in the group. He added with a smile, "Jim impresses me as one who is like John Wayne. Now don't get me wrong, I like John Wayne, and Jesus was the original John Wayne, but Jim, you just ain't no John Wayne."

Everyone laughed good-naturedly, and when I looked across the room at Alecia, the beautiful girl with long dark hair and sparkling eyes, I saw that she was looking at me and smiling. Michael had introduced her to me earlier. I was certain that her name meant *beautiful woman*. Right now, I needed someone like her to be my friend.

God, thank you for her! How I needed someone to be nice to me. Please don't let me cry in front of these people. How will they ever understand my need for love and intimacy? I scarcely understand it myself. Is all this needing to be loved coming from the devil to distract me?

I just didn't know anymore.

"All right now, Jim came here for a special reason. He's in trouble, and I want Jim to share his story with us, and then we are going to help him. Jim, my buddy, the floor is all yours."

Silence fell over the entire room. All I could hear was breathing. Even the constant sirens that blare at all hours in New York City had stopped. Suddenly it was scary quiet.

"I...ah...offended a gang leader, one who I am working with. I embarrassed him in front of his gang—accidentally. Actually, I just lost it, and shouted at him, and called him names. I'm a little surprised he didn't kill me right there.

"As you know, the city has a job program. Well, the gang I'm working with was given the job of working in an elementary school. It was a stupid job. There were twenty-two of us, and all we were allowed to do was empty a few trashcans and wash the chalkboards. Day after stupid day, their stupid job was to wash the chalkboards. It didn't take long for people to get bored and start fooling around.

"One thing led to another, and somebody broke a window. The janitor, who didn't like us at all and didn't want us there, threw a fit and began cussing out the guys. Eddie jumped in my face and cussed me out. The janitor told us to get out of his school, and he went to call the police.

"I got so angry at Eddie. Although I was angry at the janitor too, I was angrier at Eddie. He had just cost us the whole program. But my anger had just cost me my paychecks, which I was counting on, really counting on.

"Also, I now had to face Joey and tell him I screwed up and cost him the project. He warned me against not screwing up. I was just so full of anger; it just exploded. I now realize that I was full of a lot of pent-up anger at everyone.

"Anger is something I have tried so hard not to display. It's just a deep feeling in me, not to show any anger."

"Why do you think that is?" someone asked.

"I found out early in life that I didn't like my folks because they were always angry at me. So I looked for love and acceptance elsewhere—especially in my friends. One day I got mad at a friend and hollered at him and said some mean things. 'I don't want to be your friend no more,' he hollered back at me.

"I learned quickly that if I wanted friends, I'd better not make them angry or show anger at them. I've spent the rest of my life buying friends with kindness or money—actually buying them something.

"I've always been so afraid of losing friends, because if I do, then I have nothing left."

"So you bottle up your anger and pretend that everything is OK?"

"Yeah."

"Spent your whole life being dishonest?"

"Yeah."

I had never thought about it like that before, but it was true. I couldn't believe that I was sitting here in a room full of people I barely knew spilling my guts and letting down my defenses. I guessed that Alecia would never like a guy like me—a phony.

I got up and walked out, and went to the room where I would be sleeping. I sat on the only chair in the room and cried.

I heard the sound of someone knocking on my door. *What if it's Alecia? What will I say?*

I opened the door slowly and there stood Alecia and another girl.

"Jim, we just wanted you to know that we think you are very brave and courageous. I don't know what I would do if I were in your shoes. But, we wanted you to know that we would not think you a coward if you stayed here or went back to DC." They both smiled at me and then turned and left. I smiled to myself.

Maybe I'm not such a loser.

I felt a mixture of emotions. I could just move here and stay where it was safe, and maybe get something going with Alecia, the one with the sparkling eyes, or I could just go home, back to college, and maybe write a book. It really wasn't necessary for me to go back to face Eddie. Hey, how long can guilt last anyway?

But there was an even bigger issue bothering me: if I didn't go back, what would that mean for the Young Life work there? Would it mean that I really was a phony? Would that send Eddie and the gang the message of "come to Jesus and He will take care of you"—that is, unless you just happened to be a dishonest white boy who was now running for his life, afraid to trust the God he talked about. But this was no small issue! **This was my life!**

Could I really trust God to protect me?

I didn't know. I just didn't know anymore.

CHAPTER 13

Sitting on a bench in front of their building—the bench that nobody else dared to sit on—were Eddie and Carmen.

Eddie stared into space. He took a long drag on his cigarette then puffed out smoke rings.

"Y' know, Sis, sometimes I get tired of being Eddie."

"Yeah, I know what you mean; sometimes I get tired of being 'virgin Carmen.'"

Spinning around, Eddie put his face nose to nose to hers and said, **"Don't get so smart, woman; remember, I could have you killed in a second**." He snapped his fingers for emphasis. "Lots of my guys would jump at the chance to hurt someone, especially someone close to me, if they thought they could get away with it."

Carmen jumped to her feet and screamed, "**You pig! I hate you!**"

"Sit down, girl; y' know I'm only messin' with you. I would torture badly anyone who ever hurt you. And don't ever say you are tired of being a virgin. What? Do you want to be a slut just like all these other women?"

"What about your precious girlfriend?" Carmen demanded. "Is she a slut? You sleep with her, don't you?"

"Watch your mouth! We men are different—we need sex."

"Oh, and we don't?"

Eddie took a long slow drag on his cigarette. "Tell me again. I'm not sure what I just heard." Eddie glared at Carmen.

"You heard me all right. You just gotta grow up."

Eddie exploded. "**Don't do it, Sis. Don't push me!**"

"I'm scared for you, Eddie."

"He's a man of God—for God's sake, Eddie, what will God do to you if you kill his man?"

Pacing around the bench, Eddie said, "Don't you think it scares me too?

Eddie took another long drag on his cigarette. Sweat was pouring down his face.

"What can I do? He embarrassed me. He put me down in front of my boys. They'll lose respect for me, or worse. He's put me in a very bad spot. It's all his fault—I hate Jim."

"Eddie, maybe you should talk to Joey. He's a pretty smart man. Maybe he can help you figure out a way to save face and still not kill Jim."

"What you saying—that such a man as me should run to some other man to ask advice? Are you crazy?"

"You say you are worried about what your boys will think. I think maybe you ought to worry about what they think or feel about you killing Jim. You know, to some of them he's like a priest—a man of God. You know what they would say if you was planning on killing a cop down here."

Eddie put out his cigarette and then took another out of his pack. Putting the pack back in his pocket, he tamped the cigarette against his hand, stuck it in his pocket, and pulled out a match. He struck the match against his foot but it didn't light. He struck it against his foot again and again, but it wouldn't light.

"What is this—is the whole world against me?"

Crumbling the cigarette in his hand, he rolled and rolled the tobacco into tiny balls and then swallowed all of it. "There. That'll do it."

"Eddie, there is something else you need to know about Jim. I love him. I've loved him since the first day you introduced him to me. He's not like the other boys; he's a real man."

Eddie stopped pacing.

He froze right where he stood.

He didn't move.

Then turning slowly, Carmen saw that his whole face had changed as if he'd become a monster.

His eyes now wild and fierce, and his breathing was fast and shallow.

Carmen was suddenly frightened—extremely frightened—not of some stranger, but of her own brother. She felt panicked. She should have kept quiet.

"**You Puerto Rican whore**!" Eddie's eyes spewed pure hatred.

"**I'm not a whore**."

"**You slimy witch**!" Eddie flew into a rage. Charging like a wild bull, he raced straight at the bench—straight at his sister.

"So, he's been screwing my own sister right behind my back? Now I'll kill him for sure."

She panicked, her thoughts racing in desperation.

What should I do?

Should I run for my life?

Am I about to die? Here? All alone? Oh Jim, what have I done?

All of a sudden, a strange feeling came over her. *I must not die here tonight…I must fight Eddie with everything in me.*

Rising up quickly from the bench, Carmen confronted Eddie. "*You got it all wrong. He never touched me.* He knows from the way I look at him that I care about him, but he's never even tried to kiss me. I long for him just to hold me in his arms, but he won't out of respect for you. Not only does he respect you, but for some crazy reason that I don't understand, he loves you like a brother. I think he might even take a bullet for you."

Eddie took a step closer to his sister. "Oh, yeah? First, he disgraces me, and then he sneaks around with my sister behind my back. The man has no honor." The sweat beaded up on his forehead; his face had already turned a deep red.

"You know better than that. You're just so irate that you don't want to know the truth. The truth is that it's your pride that has caused all these problems—not Jim."

Eddie glared at his sister for a moment then stared off into the darkening sky. It was getting ready to rain. Thank God—he could end this horrible conversation with his sister and go somewhere to try to figure things out.

"I gotta go," he said, and he started to walk away.

"**Don't you move, Eddie! Don't you dare walk away from me!** I won't let you kill the only man who has ever treated me respectfully and offered me a dream of being something more than just Eddie's kid sister. No sir, you ain't going anywhere. **You so set on killing someone, kill me! Kill me! Eddie. Kill me!**"

Dropping to the ground, she cried out, "I don't want to live without Jim. I don't even want to be your sister anymore. Was a day when I was proud to be your sister—but not anymore! So go ahead, big man, get it over with! Kill me, and then tell everyone it's over."

Carmen burst into tears. She could feel the warm tears cascading over her soft cheeks.

Eddie reached into his right rear pocket where he had put the gun he was going to use to kill Jim. He could feel the cold hard metal. He held it tightly.

Never had anyone, let alone Carmen, his little sister who he was dedicated to protect, talked to him like that. He would definitely kill Jim—and then maybe Carmen too. He stared hard at his only sister who had now betrayed him and all he stood for.

What was going on?

Carmen got up and walked away, sobbing. Eddie paced around the bench.

"Women, you're all so complicated," he said to his sister's back. "Why can't you be simple like us men?"

Eddie sat and muttered, "Life used to be so nice and easy 'til I beat Tony and his brothers and became the leader of this stupid gang. Not like I had any choice—they were going to hurt me—but I just don't like being the gang leader anymore.

"What am I gonna do? I can't just step down; that's just not an option, yet I know that someday, somebody is gonna challenge me, and I will have to kill him or be killed. What a miserable life I lead."

Now what? Eddie groaned as three guys walked toward him.

CHAPTER 14

Here comes that stupid Tony and his brothers. He's been pissed at me ever since I embarrassed him last week in front of everyone. But how many times have I told him to leave the Italians alone? No, last week he tried to have sex with one of their women, and it nearly started a war between us. Yeah, I beat him bad. He is lucky I didn't kill him. Next time, I WILL KILL HIM. I suspect he really wants me dead so he can be the leader.

"Yo, what's up?" Tony called out as he approached Eddie.

Eddie eyed Tony suspiciously, watching carefully to see where his two brothers were standing. If they had come for a fight, he was ready. Slowly, so as not to show any fear, Eddie rose from his bench, turned, and faced Tony. He took another long drag on his cigarette and blew his smoke directly at Tony, a gesture to show not only his power, but his disgust for Tony and his brothers. He hated the fact that all three of them were fellow Puerto Ricans, bound by blood, since most were interrelated.

Staring directly into Tony's eyes, Eddie took two steps closer and blew more smoke into Tony's face.

"Whadda you want, loser?"

Tony's brothers started to close in on Eddie, but Tony raised his hand signaling them to stop. Tony walked past Eddie and took a seat on Eddie's bench.

Smiling, Eddie laughed and said, "Oh, so youse guys came here to die?"

Tony stretched out his feet and leaned back. "Eddie, I come here to make a truce between us. It ain't right that cousins should disrespect each other like we do, so what you say we shake and be friends?"

"Friends? Friends? Youse guys tried to kill me."

Rushing to where Tony sat, Eddie pulled him up and shoved him into his brothers. Tony fell down, sat and looked at Eddie, then motioned for his brothers to help him up. Standing, Tony took out a pack of cigarettes, slowly pulled one out, took a match from his pocket, and struck on the cover. He lit his cigarette and took a long draw.

"C'mon, guys, let's get out of here before I really get mad."

Eddie chuckled as they strutted away. "Hurry up, losers, before I ask my sister to kick your asses."

Without turning around, Tony extended a lone finger back at Eddie.

Oh boy, as if I don't have enough to worry about, now I gotta watch my back for those punks. Well, for now, they're scared that I could really hurt one or all of them, and they should be. Nothing would give me greater pleasure than beating them in front of their mother and sisters. I can just see it now, breaking their arms, stomping on their legs and several good kicks to their heads while their mommas cry for me to stop. Nah, not worth my time, but if they keep it up....

Eddie turned and walked toward the Manhattan River, a dirty stinky river full of trash and dead fish, but it was "their" river." He looked across the water toward Brooklyn. *Brooklyn is a crazy place, not like here. Here we have peace and quiet, and I enforce it. Nobody hurts anybody unless I say so. Over there, man people are always killing each other, even Puerto Ricans killing Puerto Ricans. Bad, man, bad.*

God, Eddie thought to himself, *what can I do to make my life better? Right now, my life is horrible. No real friends that I can trust, my girl wanting me to get her pregnant so she can have kids and collect welfare money…hmm, three kids and she would be rich off welfare. No, now is not the time. If I am going to be a father, I want to be a good father, not like my old man. Drunken bum! 'Sides, I want me a classy woman, not any project whore.*

CHAPTER 15

High up on the roof, forty-seven stories above ground, Carmen watched her brother as he "talked" with Tony and his brothers. She feared for him, she feared him, and she loved him. Standing alongside her was Skamp, her cousin. They had been there for maybe thirty minutes. Watching Eddie confront Tony and his brothers sent a chill down Carmen's spine. She shook violently for a moment. Observing Eddie from this distance took away some of her fear of him. He looked just like any other person, except he walked with a very slow deliberate bearing as if he were the King of Kings. Too bad his gang wasn't called "the Kings."

The roof had a three-foot-high wall around the perimeter. She and Scamp came up here lots of times and just leaned on it and watched the traffic below. Tonight their eyes followed Eddie. They watched as he walked down to the river's edge and started casting stones into the slow-moving water. In the shimmering moonlight, they could just barely make out the ripples slowly moving away from where the stones had splashed.

Carmen turned to her cousin and just studied her.

"What?" Scamp laughed and shook her head.

"I just wish…."

"Yeah? Sometimes I just wish too."

"No, it's not like that. Sometimes I just wish I was you."

"Are you crazy, cuz? Me? Girl, you have no idea what my life is like these days."

"Mmm, yeah, it's just that being lil' Miss Perfect, lil' virgin Carmen is no easy ride either."

"I hear you, but don't ever, ever let Eddie hear you say that, cause, honey, I'm afraid he really would kill you."

Turning away from Scamp, Carmen said, "You've had so many lovers. I've had none. Just once, I'd…."

"You'd what? Give it up to some guy willing to pay you five bucks? Honey, everything I do, I do for one reason only: for the money. I do it to survive! Sex with these boys means nothing to me. I don't feel a thing. Now you, you got Jim, only he don't know it yet, but when he does, girl, look out! That man is going to explode your life."

Laughing Carmen replied, "I only wish that were true, but he is a man of God. So far, not even trashy Teresa with her tight pants and low-cut T-shirts has been able to snag him."

"Dat's because, honey, he is saving himself for you. I've seen the way he looks at you, and so has Frankie. If he is not more careful, one of these days, even Eddie's gonna see him; then I don't know what is gonna happen."

"Oh, if only I could be sure. If I was sure, I could wait and wait, but until then…."

"One of these days, you'll get a signal from him, of that, I am sure."

"I hope so," Carmen said.

"Gotta run, honey." Scamp hugged Carmen for a long time.

Carmen walked over to one of the benches on the roof, buried her head in her hands, and just cried and cried. Her long hair covered her face so that no one passing by would know she was crying, but what would the sister of Eddie have to cry about after all?

"Oh, God, is there really a God? Joey says so, and now Jim comes into our neighborhood and says so. I've never seen or met a man like Jim. Everyone loves him, even Eddie, though he would never admit it. I am so tired of not being loved, so tired of being Eddie's little sister, so tired of life. Please, God, if you are real, please help me. I have done all the good things that Joey and Jim says we should do, but still, I am so lonely." Standing up and walking back to the wall at the edge of the roof, she looked for Eddie, but didn't see him. It was too dark now. She broke into a song. "I'm just a lonely girl, lonely and blue, I'm all alone with no one to love, please, please God, let someone love me, I'm all alone, so sad and so lost."

She stopped singing and heaved a deep sigh of resolution. "Tomorrow, I will send Scamp to bring Jim to me. My heart is breaking. I just got to know, do I have any chance with him. Me, a Puerto Rican with a white boy, a college boy—I must be out of my mind, but I got to know!"

CHAPTER 16

A soft knock brought me back to reality. With a trembling hand, I opened the door. There stood Michael. He had a concerned look in his eyes. His smile was a sad one; in fact, it was barely a smile.

"Jim, I heard what you said just now before I knocked. Correct me if I'm wrong, but I heard you say that being loved was important to you, and being intimate before you die was very important to you. Is that correct?"

I could feel the pain welling up deep within me. I was terrified that anyone might find out my deep, dark, dirty secret. Christians aren't supposed to want sex before marriage. Everybody talked about it and said how great it was, but I wanted to know for myself.

Tears were struggling to burst forth. An overwhelming sense of vomiting right there was taking over my body. Fear had locked a death hold on me—cold hard FEAR.

Could I tell Michael?

How could I tell Michael?

Would a guy like him, clean cut, happily married, never knowing the struggles I faced, could he possibly understand? I just didn't see how. Truth is, I was facing death either way: death at the hands of Eddie or the death of my vision of myself—a hero turned coward.

No, this was possibly my last chance, and possibly—just possibly—God might lead Michael to understand.

My faith was being shattered.

It was time I said something.

"Michael …I'm not sure where to start. It's such a long story. All my life, love, intimacy, and fun have always been linked together. In high school, there was a lot of joking about sex. One day, my mother overheard me talking to someone on the phone about sex, and when she heard me mention the word, she exploded. She smacked me upside my head and threatened to beat me within an inch of my life if ever she found out that I was doing that. It was for marriage she said.

"I still didn't know what it was, but I knew that many of the boys and girls in school were drinking beer, smoking cigarettes, and doing it. They all said it was so much fun. Several times some of the girls asked me if I was still a virgin.

"It frightened me because I knew that my mom meant it when she said she would beat me badly. I didn't know what to do.

"When I became a Christian, I was told that it was for marriage, and that it was an unpardonable sin for a young man like me to do it. I thought that it was an act between two people who loved each other—not just some guy and some girl. Boy, I was really confused.

"When I met Stella, my high school girlfriend, I asked her at one point about being intimate. After all, we loved each other very much and probably were going to get married. She was horrified. Then she got really angry with me and told me that she was not that type of girl. We finally smoothed things out.

"Now here I am, twenty-five years old and about to die, and I've never experienced having someone really love me enough to share their most prized possession with me.

"I figured that for a girl to consent to share her secret parts with me, and that's what I called it, because I never saw it, she would have to love me in a very special way.

"Then I come to New York City, and everyone seems to be having fun except me. Everyone is drinking beer, smoking weed, doing drugs, and having so much fun–except me. Me, I'm miserable—and I'm about to die miserable.

"Basically, I've always associated intimacy with the fact that someone really loves me enough to share it with me and something that is so much fun. Am I wrong?"

Michael had sat there on a soft stool next to a larger chair and listened to me the whole time without moving. His expression had changed from a questioning look to one of great sympathy. His face looked pained for my sorrow. His eyes looked down at the floor. Slowly he raised his head.

"I don't know what to tell you, Jim. First of all, I want to assure you that I heard every word you said, and that it will go no farther than this room—OK?"

I nodded my head slowly and took a deep breath of relief. I realized that I had been speaking very fast and was now worn out.

"Jim, you're not the first fellow to feel this way, and you probably won't be the last. I don't know if that makes you feel any better, but what you are struggling with is reality. So many of us grow up without ever really experiencing real love."

"So you come here among the really down-and-outs, people who need someone to love them—to find love and acceptance. But they still can't offer you what you are seeking."

"Yes." I felt so confused and embarrassed.

"I'm afraid that God is the only one who can truly offer you the love you are seeking. I don't mean to sound as if you are doomed, but even if Carmen gave you sex, you would find it hollow, because you are looking for love and not just sex—really. What do you think?"

"I don't know what to think anymore, Michael. I don't know if even God can give me the love I seek."

"Why don't we pray together, Jim?"

"I just don't know that prayer holds any answers for me, Michael. I think I'd just rather be alone right now. I don't even know if I want to live any longer."

CHAPTER 17

"Oh, God," I cried, collapsing to my knees and grabbing hold of the edge of the bed. "**I don't want to die**. Why do I have to be so different from everyone else? Why can't I have a girlfriend? Why can't I have fun like they do? Why can't I just be like one of them? I just don't understand. **Why do I have to die? Why, God? Why?**"

I lay on the bed and sobbed. I felt so lost. I had come to rescue "these people," "these sinners." Somehow, it seemed like I was the one who needed rescuing. I wanted so desperately to be liked and loved, yet here I was, always the outsider. People would say to me, "Jim, I want to be a Christian, but I just can't be the Christian that you are."

I used to take such pride in the fact that I was so much better than they were. I was white, educated, a spiritual leader. I was free. I could pick up tomorrow and go home or go anywhere I wanted, but they were stuck in the projects. But now, everything was so confusing.

Perhaps I was the one who really needed help. Perhaps I was the real prisoner. Just maybe they were better than I. At least they weren't being phony.

They were the real thing. They weren't pretending to be somebody they weren't. They were having all the fun, and I was having none.

I lay there a long time. Suddenly it occurred to me that I was a fraud, a bigot, a man pretending to be an equal whenever it suited me, but with an escape clause."

What then was this all about, God? Why did I give up all my middle-class comforts to come here and live in this pigsty, if you aren't for real? Was it for the glory? What glory?

Tomorrow I could be dead, and none of my Christian friends back home would know of my sacrifice. If they heard about it at all, they would just hear that I was killed by some gangster, not that I died a "hero."

Hero—me, a hero? No, more like a fraud.

Perhaps a lot like you, God!

Where have you been when I've needed you? Where are you now?

Have I been a fool all these years to give up all the pleasures of this world to follow a God that really doesn't exist?

Have I been a fool?

Am I a fool?

Do you really exist, God?

The sounds of sirens from police cars racing by interrupted my praying and struggling.

Hmm, there'll be no police cars racing to save me. The police rarely come into our neighborhood—except with an escort.

The thought of the silliness of the whole ridiculous situation made me smile.

What was life all about?

What was I all about?

No one really cared if these kids lived or died or got saved. They were the throwaways, the dropouts of society, the violent drug users no one wanted to touch or have in their neighborhood.

Why was I wasting my life here? Would my life or death make any difference?

I'd sacrificed my entire young adult life to live like a good Christian. I'd never smoked, consumed alcoholic beverages, or been with a woman—all because the church told me that as a Christian I was not to do these things. Jesus would not be pleased. I wouldn't go to heaven.

How true were all these things really?

CHAPTER 18

Here I was about to die and I'd never really known what it was like to be loved—truly loved just for being me.

Not I, the mighty Christian leader, but me—just me.

Before I could stop them, the tears came again. They burned all the way deep down into my very soul.

I did not know if there were any answers.

I did not know where I would go from here or what I would do. Perhaps my whole life had been just that, a fraud. I fell asleep.

When I awoke, I felt that a strange peace and calmness had come over me, just like the night I asked Jesus to come into my life. That night too I had wrestled with God, only on a much smaller scale.

I lay there awhile before moving. "Is that you, God?" I asked out loud. There was no answer—just silence.

I found my mind returning to the Bible and the things I had learned about the God I had given my life to serve—and possibly really *given* my very *life* to serve.

God had also loved the unlovely, the rejects of this world. In fact, God had sent His only Son to die for people who were treating Him as their enemy. God loved people, and I loved these same people. Just maybe God had fashioned my heart for such a time as this.

Maybe God and I were a lot alike. Both of us love these people— both of us for the same reasons. Both of us want these people to return our love. Both of us get angry when they don't. The God of the Old Testament would get very angry.

Perhaps I really was "called" by God, whatever that meant, to give my life for these people. It didn't make a whole lot of sense to me, but for some reason, I had a strange peace about everything.

Oh God, help me to love these people, all these people. I don't know how to. I need you to love them through me. Please let me be your vessel. May they see more of you and less of me.

CHAPTER 19

J im, can we talk? Just you and I?"

Sitting across from me was Dianna, Michael's wife. We were just finishing breakfast.

"Michael told me more about your struggles, and I'd like to help."

Puzzled and still very much confused, I hesitantly accepted her offer. "I guess."

"Let's go into the kitchen where we can talk privately," she said.

What a difference from the place where I lived. We had no separate kitchen, just a microwave and a sink. This kitchen reminded me of the home I grew up in, and immediately I felt a sense of peace.

Mom...oh, Mom, what have I done? I broke your heart when I dropped out of college and moved to his vicious city, a city of sin and darkness. Oh, Mom, I feel so alone...so all alone.

"Jim, Michael told me about your struggles and especially that you're confused about what to do. He said that you feel so lost and lonely—is that correct?"

"Yes…I am very lost and lonely."

I looked away from her.

"Spiritually shot, maybe even dead?" asked Diana.

I scooted my chair back and laid my head on the kitchen table.

Dianna came around the table and rubbed the back of my neck. "Jim, Michael told me that you love this girl Carmen, is that correct?"

Without moving, just enjoying the kind, loving attention I was getting from such a caring person, I muttered, "Yeah."

"Tell me about her."

"Carmen? She's incredible. She's the prettiest, sweetest, happiest, most easygoing lovable girl I've ever known. When I'm near her, I feel like I'm ten feet tall, invincible, a champion and a real man. I do love her, more and more each day. I would love to spend the rest of my life with her."

"How does she feel about you?"

"She says that she loves me too. And when she kissed me—wow! My whole world exploded in joy."

"Sounds like you got a case of a 'love Jones'—you're hooked on her."

"Yeah, she's so cool. She makes life worth living."

"Then why don't you marry her?"

I sat back in my chair, stretched, then got up and walked around the table to a window. Looking out the window, I said, "I can't."

Diana had no idea what a raw nerve she had just hit. I felt as if my blood was draining from me.

"Why not?"

"There are a couple of really big reasons, the first and most important being that her brother Eddie is going to kill me. There is no doubt about that.

"Secondly, even if he didn't kill me for embarrassing him in front of his gang, he surely would kill me if he knew that I wanted to marry his sister. He's very protective of her, and nobody—but nobody—gets to date her.

"Thirdly, even if we managed to run away together somewhere, I don't have a job and she has no skills. I could never support her. I couldn't take her away from her family. I love her, but there's no future for us."

"I see what you're saying. You're in a dangerous dilemma. I don't know what else to say except may God go with you."

"Yeah, I don't know either. I truly wish things were different. I wish I didn't have to die. When I gave my life to Jesus, I had no idea that one day he would ask me to die for him."

Picking up the coffeepot, I poured myself a small cup of coffee and drank it down quickly. "Gotta go; thanks, Dianna. Pray for me."

Lord, either I am a fool, or somehow, I am your messenger. I don't know which!

CHAPTER 20

Eddie what I'm saying is, you know Jim—he's so cocky sometimes. That's one of the reasons he fits in with you guys so well. He just made a mistake. I'm asking you to forgive him. He gave up so much just to come here and help you and your boys."

"Give me a break." Eddie said.

Eddie stared hard at Joey, his cold steely eyes trying to intimidate him while he pulled out a pack of cigarettes.

"I dunno, Joey...I mean, you know I like Jim, but he humiliated me."

Eddie paced back and forth in front of his bench. Joey just sat there quietly.

"What can I do?" Eddie said. "I can't just let him get away with that—right? Then every punk in the neighborhood would disrespect me. I'd have to kill a lot of guys just to get that respect back. So tell me, what am I gonna do?"

"I see your predicament," Joey said. "But I just can't stand by and watch you kill Jim, either."

Eddie leaned in close, his face just inches from Joey's. He stared hard into Joey's eyes.

"Yeah, well there's nothing you can do to stop me."

"You're right. There is nothing I can do to stop you. That's why I'm here now—to ask you not to do this terrible thing."

Eddie turned and started to walk away. He waved his hand sideways as if to dismiss Joey.

"Eddie, I want you to think about something," Joey called after him. "Are you happy? I mean really happy? One thing about Jim is that he loves you, and he is the one guy who could rescue you from this hellhole you live in. There is no one else! Only Jim cares enough, and only he has the resources."

Eddie stopped sauntering and turned around. "It's too late for me, Joey; no one can help me now. I gotta do what I gotta do, and that's that."

"Eddie!" Johnny came running up. "I heard Joey say that Jim's coming home tonight."

Jim, why don't you just stay up there? It's all your fault, but I'm the one who is suffering.

CHAPTER 21

The train ride home was a long one.

Sitting on a seat in the back of the train, I tried to hide my face from everyone. I just felt like they all knew that I was running from Eddie and he would somehow hurt me.

Crazy, but that's where I was struggling with my emotions.

Part of me was afraid. Part of me just wanted to get it over with.

I was glad that Joey had sent me to Michael's.

If this was to be my last day alive, I was glad I had the time with Michael and the Lord.

If I had to die—well, then my life had been a short one.

But, I'd had a lot of fun, and had experienced a lot that many others my age had never experienced.

On the other hand, if for some reason I didn't die—maybe, just maybe, Carmen and I could have a life together.

Never had I met a girl like her. She wasn't like most of the girls in the projects. I hated to sound judgmental, but most of them acted like tramps. Carmen was a diamond in the rough—a rare find.

Perhaps we could make a go of it. I didn't know how, but just possibly, some miracle would happen. What would life be like with Carmen? Hmm…. Just then I saw in my mind five little Jimmy's and Carmen's running around our apartment. Ha, ha!

The subway would start off slow, suddenly speed up, sway violently from side to side, and then abruptly screech to a quick halt with a thud.

People jumped up and poured out the doors. New people began streaming in.

Suddenly, I realized that I was there—home—my stop.

I got up and raced out the door into the vast crowd pushing its way down the platform and up the stairs. The bright sunlight hit me as I exited the stairs.

Well, here I am!

Life will never be the same.

This is definitely going to be a game changer!

CHAPTER 22

I t was only a couple of blocks back to my apartment, yet as I walked along, it seemed like everyone was staring at me, like they was waiting to see what would happen next.

The assurance that I would be all right was fading fast.

When I arrived at my place, I stopped at the bottom of the concrete steps.

As I looked up at the building, I remembered my first time standing there at the bottom of those steps, staring up.

Much had happened since then—and I was a different guy now.

This time there was no drunk sitting on the steps, no Frankie and Clarkie coming out the door to rescue me.

Just me—standing there.

A wave of panic surged through me. *What if...?*

Well, here we go I thought to myself as I slowly walked up the stairs. Reaching the top, I stopped at Joey's apartment and knocked softly on the doorframe.

"Come in," I heard Joey's voice calling from his office in the back. I took a deep breath. What kind of mood would he be in? What had transpired since I left? What was waiting on the other side of the door? *Oh God, here I am.*

I walked in and took a seat opposite Joey.

"So, *compadre—Buenos Dias.*" Joey rose, walked over to me, and reached out his hand to shake mine. "Welcome back. Did you have a good rest?"

I shook his hand and smiled. That doggone Joey. He just had a wonderful way of putting me in a good mood. Somehow, when he was with me, everything seemed OK.

"Ready to face Eddie?"

Mimicking Joey's famous raising of his eyebrows to express himself, I tried to raise mine.

"Well, that's the reason I came back. I hope I did the right thing… but I really don't want to die."

He shook his head slowly, and I watched as his expression had changed from a humorous one to one of concern. "Sure you want to go through with this? You don't have to, y' know."

The softness of the chair made me just want to go to sleep. I just sat there and relaxed for a couple of moments. Shrugging my shoulders, I replied, "I don't know, Joey. I just don't know. But, here I am—no more running.

I did Eddie wrong, and now I'm ready to pay the price. Funny thing, we talk so much about loving Jesus—but when it comes time to die and go be with him—forever—we chicken out.

"I've given it a lot of thought and I'm no longer afraid. 'Yea, though I walk through the valley of death'—well, it's my turn now." I smiled.

Joey laughed. "I'm glad you can be happy or at least relaxed. I'm not so sure I'd be so ready." He sat there and just gazed at me. "So what's your plan?"

"*Plan*? I got no plan." I laughed. "Maybe I'll go down to the projects and say, "Hey Eddie, it's time—you ready to kill me? Or hey, Eddie, you kill me." I laughed again.

"You definitely are one sick puppy, Jim." Joey laughed.

"Yeah—what other choice do I have?"

I rose and walked to the door. "Y' know, Joey, I've learned a lot in the last couple of days. I've grown a lot too. Mistakes, man, have I made a lot. If I get the chance, I'd like to straighten a lot of things out."

"Well, good luck. We'll be praying for you."

"Yeah, thanks."

CHAPTER 23

I t was a long walk down to the projects, but today it seemed even longer. I was on my way to meet Eddie and end this once and for all. Joey had said he would go with me, but I said no. I had to do this myself.

Wait! Wait! For God's sake, stop!

Each step took me one step closer to my destiny—in this case, my death.

You don't have to do this.

You don't have to die!

This incessant voice grew louder and louder in my head. A raging war was coursing throughout my entire being.

I stopped for a moment. My heart was beating so fast, I had a hard time breathing.

My mind was fighting for survival; my heart was leading me toward suicide.

If I did not stop now, turn around, and run away, it would soon be too late.

A whole year of relationship building, days and months of allowing these guys to play jokes at my expense, all of it for this one reason: to build solid relationships with them that would allow me to tell them the good news about how much God loves them.

Now it was all blown away—in an instant!

Me and my foolishness—I just couldn't leave well enough alone.

No! I always had to be right!

Now, I must pay the ultimate price at the hands of a man who once was my best friend.

Oh, God, I don't want to die.

Too late now. I saw Eddie and his gang waiting for me.

CHAPTER 24

Walking, actually staggering, slowly towards me, we were surrounded by a large crowd who had come to see me executed

"Why, Jim? Why did you have to go and act so stupid? You leave me no choice—everybody knows that! You are my friend, Jim. Friends don't treat friends like that."

At this point Eddie was blubbering. A mixture of tears and snot were flowing down his face. In his hand, he still held his gun.

It may have only been a small .25 caliber gun, but as I stared down the barrel, it looked like a cannon. Boy was I scared.

Still shaking ferociously, he took the last and final step toward me where he now stood just inches from me. He tapped my chest with his gun.

Suddenly, all fear left me, and all that remained was a deep remorse for the trouble I had caused.

"Eddie," my voice squeaked, "I'm so sorry for the trouble I caused you. You were right, and I was wrong to interfere. Do what you have to do—I'll still love you."

Unexpectedly, Eddie staggered back a couple of steps, uncocked his gun, and put it in his pocket.

Stepping forward again, he lunged at me. Before I could move, he wrapped his arms around me.

"I love you, Jim. I can't kill you. You're more than just a friend. You are a big part of my life."

At that, Carmen rushed over and wrapped her arms around both of us and just cried.

Slowly the crowd who had gathered to see me executed melted away. Only a few stayed behind.

Eddie, Carmen, and I walked over to the park and sat down on a bench. Carmen went to get us a couple of sodas. Eddie just lay back against the supports of the bench.

"We got a lot to talk about, Jim."

"Yeah, so I figure. I'm real sorry for all the trouble I caused you."

"Yeah, well you should be. And by the way, I know about you and Carmen too."

CHAPTER 25

That really took me by surprise. How did he know? Who talked? How much did he know? Slowly I could feel fear trying to creep in once more. Had I just survived one killing only to face being killed again? *Oh God—when will it end?*

"Thought you'd put one over on me, did you? Sneaking around behind my back—I *trusted* you, Jim. You sleep with her? Huh? Come on, might as well tell me everything now—while I'm too drunk to kill you."

Careful Jim—be careful what you say and how you say it.

"No Eddie, it's not like that. I love her, and I think she loves me too."

He leaned over so close and held his head just inches from mine. I could see his bloodshot eyes clearly. The stench of alcohol emanating from his breath was almost enough to make me drunk.

"Yeah . . . well love here means babies."

"Well, not for us—at least not right away. I gotta get myself squared away and get a real job. She wants to finish high school. Eddie, we do want to get married; we just want to do it right—y' know, a church wedding, a honeymoon, a house over in Jersey. I want her to be proud to be my wife and raise a bunch of little Jimmy's and Carmen's."

"Little Jimmy's." Eddie snickered.

CHAPTER 26

Carmen returned with the sodas. Eddie sat back and leaned away from me.

"Well, I just might have something to say about all that," Carmen interjected. She'd heard the last bit of our conversation. "First, I do love Jim." Carmen smiled at me. "But, marriage is out for now. I just want to have lots of babies by Jim—now."

At that, Eddie came up off the bench quickly. "**What?**"

Carmen put her arm around her big brother. "Relax, big brother, just messing with your mind. Jim and I never got the chance to talk about us yet. It's late, time for us to go home. You too, Jim, go home and get some rest. We'll talk tomorrow."

She pulled Eddie in tight to her and they walked toward the project. Eddie was stumbling. I started to grab Eddie and help Carmen carry him home.

"No, just go, Jim, I got Eddie. Go home. See you tomorrow." It was a funny scene. Big Eddie, who was always in control, being guided by the arms of his kid sister; fortunately, it was only two blocks to their project.

I turned and walked the ten blocks back to my place. So much had happened. I really had expected to die—to be killed. It was almost anticlimactic to still be alive.

So Eddie knows about Carmen and me—now what?

Man, some sleep would be great just about now. I was so tired I could hardly walk.

The blocks pasted by slowly. When I finally got home to my apartment, everyone was there. They were still deep in prayer for Eddie and me.

"Welcome home!" they shouted. The whole building seemed to come out of their doors all at the same time.

"All right, gather around, Jim's got a long story to tell us. Some of you know parts—now we learn the whole story, right Jim?"

"Not tonight, guys. I am so tired. Sleep has my name, and it's calling me." I turned and stumbled into the bedroom and crashed into the land of sleep. *Tomorrow will be a better day. Yippee!*

CHAPTER 27

"Joey, can I talk with you?" Eddie stood at the open doorway to Joey's apartment.

"Come on in. What's on your mind?"

Eddie walked over to the coffeepot, poured himself a cup of coffee, and sat on the couch. "I need to talk to you about Jim, Carmen, and me."

"Why don't you start with you first?"

Eddie sighed deeply. He took a sip of coffee. "Joey, I'm tired of being who I am. I see myself as a loser, and I want to change. Someday, some other dude is going to challenge my leadership, and I'm either gonna to have to kill him or be killed. Either way, my life has no future."

"So what is it that you want from me?"

"I want what youse guys have—you, Jim, Clarkie, Gee, and the rest. Youse guys always seem so happy and at peace with yourself and the world. Me, every day I gotta watch my back. I can't really trust anyone. I've never felt loved …I've been so lonely. Did you know that that punk

Jim was screwing around with my sister—*my sister?* I trusted him, I believed in him, and here he was making a fool out of me. That Jim, man, he has one big set of gonads—you know what I mean? If he were one of my boys, I'd really be afraid that he was looking to replace me."

Eddie took another sip of the coffee. "Good coffee, for a white man. Not like the thick mud what us Puerto Ricans drink—but good."

"Eddie, what I hear you saying is that you want what we have. You want to be more like us—right?"

"I guess."

"Eddie, what we got is *Jesus.* We committed our lives to follow him. Sort of like your boys are committed to you and your leadership, only in a much more positive way."

"Y' know, I've heard you speak, and I listen to what Jim says, but I still don't really get it. Could you help me understand?"

"Eddie, the Bible says that no matter how good or bad a person is, in the eyes of God we are all sinners. Now what that means is that the Bible says the reason God created us was to have fellowship with him. So when we don't live in fellowship with him, we live in what God calls sin. Sin is separation from God. It means we live as if we are separated from God. Sometimes we feel that there is no God.

"This causes all kinds of sinful actions that we commit because we don't wait on God to show us how to live, you following me so far?"

"I think. I hear you saying that I need to follow someone else other than myself—like maybe God."

"Right. What you need to do is tell God that you are sorry for the bad things you have done and make a *commitment,* a promise not to do those things again, and then turn your life over to his control. Got it?"

"Not sure."

"You see, Eddie, there are two parts. The Bible calls the first repentance. That means to stop doing the wrong things in your life, including making your own decisions, and start doing the right things. Do you understand?"

"Yeah, that I can understand. I don't know if I can do it, but I do understand." Eddie said this with a big smirk.

He got up and walked over to the window. Looking out with his back to Joey, he said, "I really want to change. I just don't know how."

"Well, the good news is that God will help you and we'll help you— Jim and my boys and me. We'll be there for you every day. You want to change, and we'll be glad to help."

Joey paused before continuing. "Eddie, listen closely. Jesus loves you so much that He paid the ultimate price for you. Even when you were rebelling against him and cursing him, he allowed himself to be brutally beaten, tortured, and murdered for you. For you, he even gave up all of his friends. They didn't want him to die, but he did it anyway."

"Why? He didn't even know me." Eddie turned around and his eyes were moistened. "Why would Jesus allow himself to be hurt like that? Why didn't he fight back if he was God?"

"Because God said it was the only way to buy us back from the clutches of the evil one, Satan, the devil, y' know. Eddie, the truth is that God loves you and has a wonderful plan for your life. Do you understand that?"

"No. But if you say it's true, I believe it. What do I need to do?"

"Eddie, just close your eyes and ask God to forgive you and help you to live a good life."

Eddie walked over to Joey and put his hand on Joey's shoulder. "God, I want to be like Joey. I want you to be in my heart and life. I want to live for you. Help me. Help me to change the lives of my boys too. And God, please help Carmen to also do this."

Joey hugged Eddie and then they both cried—two warriors sharing a moment that only warriors can share.

"Why don't we go downstairs and tell Jim?"

Laughing, they went downstairs and knocked on my door. No answer. Joey inserted his key and opened the door, but when he walked in, he saw that I was not there.

"Where do you think Jim went, Joey?"

Shrugging his shoulders, Joey responded, "Don't have the foggiest."

CHAPTER 28

We sat on "our" bench, hugging and kissing. I hugged her so tightly that I thought her skinny little body might break.

"Carmen, I've done a lot of thinking. I've realized that I really do love you. You make me feel wonderful when I'm with you. When I'm here in your presence like this, I feel like a champion. I just want to jump up and beat my chest like a monkey and prance around. Do you really love me?"

Carmen didn't say anything. She just reached over and hugged me. She held me tight and then started crying softly. "Oh, Jim, I don't know when I heard such a beautiful speech. Yes! Yes, I do love you. I have waited for years for a man like you to come along. When I first met you, I just knew you were that man, but I also knew that you were unreachable for a woman like me."

We sat on a bench overlooking the river. Very few people ever wandered down there. Despite the fact that the river was a dirty brown, the air stank of sulfur from the nearby trash dumpsters and noisy birds squawked overhead, but to us it was a romantic spot.

I pulled back from our tight embrace and kissed her softly on her forehead, paused for a second then kissed her on the eyelids. It felt so good to be kissing the woman of my dreams.

Suddenly I was lost in a swirl of passion as she pulled my head lower and locked her lips on mine. *Oh, my God, what this woman does to me when she kisses me!* I'd been kissed by plenty of girls, but never like this fire and lightning that formed a mighty storm in my heart when she kissed me. I melted in her arms. I was lost in desire for her.

Carmen sat upright and smoothed out her long hair. She twisted it into a few strands. Her actions communicated to me that something was troubling her.

"Jim, I love you with all my heart. But I don't know where we go from here."

Swiftly I was brought back from my dream world to reality. Ouch, it hurt! What to do? I was lost—really lost.

Yeah, what do we do?

Marriage?

Who am I kidding?

Where would we live? How would we live?

Oh God, please God, don't take this moment from me. Don't take my dream from me. I've never felt so alive and so loved.

I sat there stunned. The silence was like the silence that often precedes a major storm. I could not think.

"Jim, honey, are you all right?"

I just sat there. I had no idea what to say.

"Jim," Carmen whispered softly in my ear. "Are you OK?"

"Carmen, I don't know what to say. I love you so much. You really complete my life. Before I met you, actually before today, my life was a mess. I was so lonely and so lost. I thought God had deserted me. But God knew what he was doing—he saved the best for last."

I held her tight. "Baby, I don't know how we are going to do it, but now that I've got you, I'll never give you up. Somehow, we'll make it. I'll need to get a real job and make some money. It could take months to save up enough to get our own place, but I'll do it. In the meantime, we can see each other every day."

I needed a moment to collect my thoughts. "Problem is…I don't want to leave, to go back to my place at nights without you. I want you always. Don't even know if I can wait 'til marriage to make love to you."

"Well, let's do it—now."

"I can't."

"What? What do you mean, you can't?"

"Honey, you know that I am a Christian."

"So?"

"Well, as a Christian, I believe in the Bible as my guidebook. The Bible says that we have to wait 'til we are married to have sex."

"Why? That sounds really silly to me. Why would a good and loving God say that?"

"I don't know. I just know His Word says that. Will you trust me on this?"

"Of course, my love."

Once again, she put me in la-la land with another one of her kisses. All my fears melted away. Life was happening so fast. It was both exhilarating and scary.

I had found my true love. God had finally brought me all that I needed to feel complete. I would get a job, but I would also continue to work with Eddie and his boys, and someday Carmen and I would get married.

Life is so sweet!

I couldn't wait to tell Joey.

CHAPTER 29

Hopefully, Eddie wouldn't mind, but I wasn't so sure. Last night he'd said it was okay for Carmen and me to like each other, but he was also very drunk.

Oh, man! What would I do if he objected?

I couldn't go through another one of his death threats. I certainly wouldn't want him to hurt Carmen. In fact, I believed that he'd kill me himself if I ever hurt his Carmen.

As I walked back to my apartment, it seemed as if the birds were singing just to me. Everybody I passed smiled at me. I was in love.

A couple of times in my life, I'd thought that I was in love, but never like this. I could feel my insides wanting to burst out in song. Yes, I was certainly and hopelessly in love. If I had to stand up to Eddie, then so be it.

I took the steps leading up to the front door two by two. Breezing through the front door and into Joey's apartment, I spun around like a dancer.

"Hel-lo Joey, how's it going?" I sang.

"What did you do with the money?" Joey asked me.

"Money? What money?"

"The money your momma gave you for singing lessons. Don't give up your day job just yet."

"Oh, I don't mind. I'm in love, drenched and drowning in love. Finally, Joey, it all makes sense. I've been so lonely that all I could see was that God wasn't being fair to me. Now, I no longer matter—only Carmen's happiness matters."

"You seen Eddie?" Joey asked.

"No," "Cause he's looking for you—**got fire in his eyes**.

CHAPTER 30

I sank down onto Joey's couch. "Now what—what did I do this time—he couldn't possibly have heard of me and Carmen yet."

Fire in his eyes? Why fire? Why was it always me? Give me a break, Lord!

Joey squatted down to my eye level. "No, the fire he's got is the Holy Spirit. He ust gave his life to Jesus, and he's so excited about it. He's gone to tell everyone, Carmen and his boys. Man, I've never seen such a rapid change in a man. Boy, Jim, you should have been here."

"Eddie? My Eddie is a Christian now?"

"Yes!" shouted Joey, his face beaming.

I jumped up off the couch and started dancing around the room. "Oh, Joey, I am so deliriously happy. How could I possibly ask for anything more? Eddie was a Christian, and Carmen and I were in love. Life is so good."

Walking over to the window, I stared hard trying to imagine Eddie's face when I told him about Carmen and me.

"Where's Eddie now?" I asked.

"He's your boy; you should know." Joey just started laughing.

"My boy—my future brother-in-law and now my brother in Christ." With that, I was out the door and on my way to find Eddie and Carmen.

CHAPTER 31

S o what you're telling me is that you love this punk?"

"Yes, Eddie, I love him with all my heart. He's the most wonderful man I've ever met. You know him—you like him."

"Yeah, Carmen, I like him, but I ain't about to marry you." Eddie laughed. "I've never seen you like this before. You always seemed so levelheaded, and now here you are acting like some silly school girl with a puppy love."

Eddie and Carmen sat on his bench. He liked teasing his sister. Nothing like this had ever happened to them before.

Now they were having fun, just like two kids in elementary school playing on the playground. Carmen couldn't sit still. One minute she was sitting—the next she was jumping up and twisting her hair and walking in circles.

"Eddie, I'm so happy. Please be happy for me."

"I am happy, Sis, but I'm also worried. It's too much, too fast, too soon for me. You haven't talked about marriage or anything like that, have you? Pop will have a fit. I would need time to break it to him."

"Oh, Eddie, thank you." Carmen jumped up and gave her brother a big hug and a kiss.

"Hey, watch that."

"Does it worry you that I might think you're a good man after all?"

Eddie got up from the bench and lit a cigarette. After inhaling slowly, he exhaled and said, "I got my own news." He smiled.

Carmen was stunned. She had never seen her brother smile like this. His eyes were sparkling. She had never seen Eddie's eyes sparkling. Did he have a secret girlfriend? Did he know something about Jim that she didn't?

"Gave my life to Jesus today. I'm a new man—one of those born-again Christians. Don't know much about it, but I feel so clean and whole and loved. I can't explain it, but sex was never this good." He strutted around in a circle and blew smoke rings.

This is not my brother, she thought to herself.

"What?" Carmen just stared at him in disbelief. Never would she have expected him to become a *Christian*. Christians were good and holy people like Jim and Joey—not Eddie.

"Is this some kind of sick joke?"

Scooping her up in his arms, he said, "You just watch me—you just watch me, baby."

The gray dreary sky had never looked prettier. Even a sunny day could not be brighter than the sunshine in these two hearts.

"You should give your life to Jesus too."

"Me?" Carmen shrugged her shoulders. "I never thought I'd hear you say something like that. I dunno. It's just all too much for me; just too much."

"Too much for you? You come over here and bust my chops with this sick puppy love thing about you and Jim, and you say I'm too much. Girl, you got a lot to learn."

The two of them just stood there and looked at each other.

Suddenly, they both burst out laughing.

"Come on, I'll treat you to some pizza at Pop's."

"Sounds good to me," Carmen said with a friendly shove. They walked a little way and saw someone approaching them.

"Hey, look who's coming down to our neighborhood—the punk Jim," Eddie exclaimed as he saw me walking toward them.

"Care to join us for some pizza? You pay, punk."

"Hmm… never met any Puerto Rican who had any money."

"Careful, man, I could have my sister sent away to my cousin's in Jersey." Eddie chuckled.

One look at Carmen and my heart was racing like a fire engine on the way to a fire. My emotions were running wild, I wanted so badly to scoop her up and hold her in my arms.

She looked so gorgeous in her dirty brown sneakers, dark navy cut-offs, and bright red tank top. She looked like a goddess. But, hey, what do I know? She would look good to me in a barrel.

We walked into Pop's, and Eddie went up to the counter and ordered us some pizzas and Cokes. Quickly seizing the moment, I whispered, "Does Eddie know anything about us?"

Surprising the living life out of me as well as scaring me to death, Carmen shrieked, "YES! Yes, scaredy cat. I told Eddie, and he's gonna kill you."

She stared at me then giggled. Eddie turned around, raised his eyebrows, and gave me a big frown—then snickered. He started laughing so hard that he fell backward into the counter.

"Look at your face, fool. You look scared to death. What, you thought I would kill you? Maybe I should." He walked quickly toward me. "Yeah, maybe I should."

We stood nose to nose, waiting for the first one to blink.

Eddie shoved me quickly and hard. I fell back into one of the chairs and landed on my butt. Shocked, I looked at both of them.

"Poor boy," Carmen said. Turning she slapped Eddie hard on the chest. "Leave my man alone."

Eddie feigned being hurt. "Oh, help me, help me; my little sister is gonna beat me up because her man is a sissy." Then they both broke out laughing, pleased with themselves and their little joke.

I sat there and smiled. They were just having a good time with me, and that was okay because we were family now.

As I looked at these two, something occurred to me. "I don't know if I can handle two more people in my life who are wasted on drugs." I looked very firm. "I just don't know—maybe I shouldn't."

Then it was my turn to laugh, but I meant it.

Keeping the mood light, I looked at Eddie and said, "So, Mister Big Shot, tell me, what's this I hear about you becoming a mighty man of valor for Jesus?"

Amused, Eddie smiled and winked at Carmen. "Yeah, I decided if you can't beat 'em, join 'em. Actually, I'm pretty excited. Like I was telling Carmen, I feel like a new man—a clean and fresh new man—so clean—so fresh. It's like the old me never existed. Y' know Jim, for the first time in my life, I really don't know what to do next."

"Oh, you'll find someone to hurt, rob, or bully. You just can't change that much," Carmen countered.

"Talk to her Jim. Tell her about the great love of Jesus and how he died for her."

Shocked, Carmen stammered, "You...you can't be serious. Can he Jim?"

"Well, Carmen, honey, you've heard what Joey has said week after week about the great love of Jesus. He's told you that God loves everyone and died for all of us—remember?"

She shook her head. "This is just all too much for me. I mean, Yeah, I heard Joey say that, but Eddie?"

"What you think, that I'm too bad a person to be forgiven?"

"Yes!" Carmen exploded. Years of anger—from so many hurts—exploded. Unexpectedly, she burst into tears.

"Oh, Eddie, I'm so afraid to believe. I'm so afraid for you. I've always been afraid that someday, someone was going to walk right up to you and kill you right in front of me." She cried and cried.

"Nah, those days are over, Sis." Eddie smiled at me.

"Chill out, girl."

Walking over I held Carmen, kissing her lightly on the head.

"Eddie's right—it's over—his days of violence are over. He wants to be a new man. What about you, honey? Jesus wants you too."

The air was shattered with a loud deep voice. "Pizza's ready, Puerto Ricans. Come get your pizza and get out."

Eddie sauntered over to the counter, stared at Pop for a few minutes, smiled, gave him the money, picked up the pizza and sodas, then extended a finger in his direction as he turned around and walked out.

CHAPTER 32

Carmen and I sat in silence on our bench. We had finished our pizzas, and Eddie had gone home.

"Jim, I love you dearly." She tugged at her shirt.

When a woman loves a man, she shows it by pleasing him. Pleasing him usually means sex. Reaching over, Carmen put her arm around my shoulders and pulled me in a little closer.

"Jim, I'm no whore, no slut—you know that, honey, right? I've saved myself just for you. I want our time to be special."

I made a great effort to think this one through. The last thing I wanted to do was insult Carmen. How could she possibly understand that according to my faith, sex was to be saved for marriage?

I really loved her, and the last thing I wanted to do was hurt her. Perhaps, if she really knew Jesus, she would understand better.

"Carmen, first I want you to know that I love you very much—more than anyone else! I've never loved a woman the way I love you. You are my life—my everything! When I wake up in the morning, the first

141

thing I think about is you. I just jump out of bed, I squeezed her tightly, "fly through the air, and land in the shower. Boom, zam, I'm finished and out the door. Just can't wait to see you these days.

"Carmen, I love you so much that I want your gift to me and my gift to you to be really special, so special that I want some time to pray about it. Y' know what I mean?"

"No, I'm not sure that I do. I mean, we love each other—what is there to pray about?"

"Prayer to me is so central to my life. Let me tell you something that changed my whole life. I grew up in church; went to church every Sunday. Felt that I really knew who God was. One day I heard a man talking about how much God loved me. Well, I always knew there was a God, sorta. But, I never knew that he cared about me. This man said that this God not only loved me, but had a plan for my life."

Taking a deep breath and looking warmly into her eyes, I said, "Darling, sweetheart, what I am trying to tell you is that up to that moment. I always thought that I was in this world alone, not really loved or understood by anyone. But this man convinced me that God did exist, and not only that, but that this God knew all about me, even my bad behavior, and yet this God loved me. Finally, I had found someone who really loved me. I was thrilled! Now, I wanted to do whatever this God asked me to do, and that is why I am here in New York.

"God sent me to tell you and all your friends that he knows all about you and loves you very much. So you see, I really wanted to please him, and I was told that God said no sex before marriage. Since I met you, the very day I met you, I wanted to take you into my arms and hold you. There is something so special about you, and I believe that God brought me here just to meet you. So I don't want to let God down after all that he has done for me, yet every fiber in my body aches to make love to you. But, I must wait."

Carmen was silent. I searched her eyes and said, "Can you believe that I had always felt that if ever anyone got to know the real me, they would not like me at all?"

"I'm not sure where you are going with this conversation, but I am listening. I too have always felt all alone. I can relate to that. Secrets lie deep inside of me that I've always been afraid of anybody—even you—finding out."

She looked away from me as she said this. "In the past, I've just buried everything deep inside of me. Nobody, not even Eddie or my momma, know some of the things I've done or said—no one!"

There was fear in her voice as she talked, fear of getting caught or found out. My heart went out to her. She was indeed a precious child in need of a protector. But I knew that the protector she needed was Jesus, the one who never fails us.

I knew I would fail her. After all, I was just a man—just a human. Humans fail other humans, sometimes.

"Carmen...." I stood up and I walked a couple of feet way then turned around.

"All my life I was afraid until I met Jesus. Finally, I met someone who knew all about me and yet still loved me. I want so much for you to experience this same love and freedom. I love you, but there will be times when I will make mistakes or get angry. But the Jesus that I have come to know—he's always stood by me. And I know he will stand by you, if you give him a chance.

"When I was at that meeting, the speaker painted a picture of how they beat and tortured Jesus. He said that Jesus went through all this pain just for us, just for me. 'Even if I were the only sinner in the room or on earth,' he said, 'Jesus would have still taken this terrible beating just for me.' Wow! That blew my mind. Can you understand why I love him so?"

"I'm scared, really scared, Jim."

Without any warning, she suddenly began to sob huge tears. I was startled. Her whole body was shuddering.

I was afraid—afraid for her. What in the world could provoke such an outburst?

She bent over into a tight huddle. Rocking back and forth, she continued her intense crying.

Sitting down alongside of her, I immediately enveloped her in my arms and held her as tightly as I could.

"You don't know, Jim. Nobody knows some of the things done to me when I was little. You don't know some of the things I've done or thought. No one could forgive me for that. No one—not even God."

"I don't know what you've experienced, sweetheart. I only know that my God has forgiven me for so much. I have a feeling that he will forgive you too."

"I cannot tell you, Jim. You are my angel, my life, my love; but maybe someday."

She still would not look me in the eye.

"Carmen, my love, you don't ever have to tell me. And the good news is that Jesus already knows, and to show his love and mercy, he has sent you me. Now, I may not be much—but I'm all that God has handy now." I laughed.

Punching me in the side, she said, "Jim, you must be right. You are a wonderful man, a mighty man of God with great courage. For you to love me—maybe you are right. Maybe I should try God. What do I need to do? Will you help me, Jim?"

"Of course, just say what I say. We are going to pray to God—OK?"
"Ok."

"Jesus, I want to have the life of joy and peace. Forgive me for the things I've done wrong and help me to live a better life. Come into my heart today and be my friend. Amen."

In good spirits now, Carmen repeated the words after me. "How can this be?" She laughed. "Already I feel so much lighter. What happened to me?"

"Jesus took you at your word. In the Bible, he says, 'Come to me all of you who are carrying heavy burdens and guilt, and I will take them away and give you rest'."

"I feel it! I feel free! For the first time in years, I feel free!"

She hugged me tight and then spun around and danced.

Although I had seen others come to know Jesus personally, never had I seen someone so tremendously happy so quickly. "Oh, Jim, is this what you and Joey have been talking about? Is this what my brother Eddie was trying to tell me?"

"Yes. Yes!" I could feel my whole face bursting with a big smile. Now, not only did I have the girl of my dreams, but she was my spiritual partner as well.

God was I happy.

What more could I ask for?

Carmen and I sat there on the bench next to the river. This had become our sacred bench. Soon she fell asleep in my arms.

Unexpectedly, I sensed someone behind me.

There was a strange chill attached to the feeling.

Slowly I loosened my hold on Carmen and turned.

What I saw stunned me!

CHAPTER 33

S he looks so lovely in your arms. She told me of her great love for you."

Standing behind me was Skamp, Carmen's notorious cousin.

"Known her all my life; God, how I love that girl. When my mom died and no one would help me, she stood by me. When everyone turned their backs on me and I was forced to trade my body for drugs and food, she never deserted me."

Walking around to the front of the bench, Skamp said, "She's a champion. I'm not the only one she's helped. No one knows. Eddie suspects, but he really doesn't know. Her papa would kill her if he ever found out. Without her, I'd be dead—no doubt about it."

I knew that Carmen and Skamp were cousins and close, but it was good hearing all the wonderful things Carmen had done.

She was sound asleep, so cozy, so comfortable in my arms. Just twenty-four hours ago, she stood watching, helplessly, as her brother pointed his gun at me and slowly pulled the trigger. She didn't know if I would die that night.

Wow! So much had happened to us all.

"She and Eddie have made big changes in their lives, Skamp—just today. Both of them gave their lives to Jesus and started life fresh."

"I heard about Eddie. Word's all over the street—some rejoicing, some not so happy, and some just watching. Let's see how long it lasts. No one really believes Eddie will change. You just watch. Something will happen, and he'll go nuts and kill someone."

"I hope you're wrong. I know it'll be tough for him, but I'm going to be right there with him helping him. He's my friend. I want to see him make it."

"He's a *dog*! Skamp scowled. "Always was—always will be."

CHAPTER 34

Word soon spread of Eddie and Carmen's conversions to Jesus. Tonight was club night.

When I arrived, the place was packed. Some people were standing in the stairwell leading down to the basement room we met in.

Usually about forty kids came out to Young Life. Tonight there were about two hundred, standing room only. Joey usually liked to have plenty of room for his funny skits, but not tonight—there was no room in "the inn."

Joey started off with a joke or two and then a short prayer. We sang several songs and the crowd clapped their hands and stomped their feet in delight.

Finally, Joey motioned for everyone to find a seat somewhere. "We've got two kinda special guests tonight. Not new—but special. They each made a commitment to give their lives to Jesus, and they want you all to know why. Let's start with Eddie and then he will be followed by his sister Carmen."

There was a lot of cheering, stomping of feet, and whistling. "Go Eddie!" the crowd cheered.

Eddie got up from where he had been sitting close to the front and walked to where Joey was holding the microphone.

"Don't need no mic for you to hear me," Eddie bellowed.

The crowd roared with laughter.

"Give it to them, Eddie!" someone called out.

Eddie paused. He looked like he was a little unsure what to say next.

"I've come to a lot of these meetings, always sat in the back, and sometimes made fun of Joey or Jim or Clarkie when they spoke—not always, but sometimes. It's because I never really understood what they were trying to tell me. Tonight I want to tell you why I switched sides— why I gave my heart and loyalty to a new gang leader. His name is Jesus."

Joey walked up to Eddie and whispered into his ear. Eddie nodded and took the mic from Joey's hand. With a slight grin, he agreed that his voice was a little softer tonight.

He would use the microphone because what he had to say was important enough for Joey to ask him to speak, and he wanted to do it right.

"I don't know if all of you heard me, but I'm following a new gang leader now, and his name is Jesus. My gang is now called Christians. All my life I've been afraid. Now, I know what some of you punks are thinking when I say I've been afraid, but hear me out."

Pausing, he cleared his throat. Everyone was straining to hear his next words. The room became so quiet, you could hear the person next to you breathing. A soft cry came from my left.

Slowly, so as not to embarrass anyone, I turned my head to see who was crying. It was Carmen. Her head was bowed down. I wanted to hold her, but she was too far away from me, and there was no way, as packed as it was, that she could move.

I knew she was crying tears of joy for her big brother, standing here in front of all these hoods, admitting that he was scared, and that he had spent his whole life being scared.

She wished she had known—wished she could have been there for him.

"My father beat me bad when I was a young kid," Eddie said, "many times. As I got older, I vowed no one would ever beat me again. I swore that no one would ever break my heart again. I loved my father when I was young, but he didn't love me."

Eddie paused and blinked his eyes. He felt tears coming.

"No matter what I did to try and win his approval, he always made fun of me and beat me. One day when he went to hit me, I grabbed his arm and spun him around behind me. I moved so fast and used so much force that I heard his arm snap. He cried out in pain. It made me sad. I should have felt guilty or something, but I didn't. I felt free! For the first time in my life, I felt free of him. He dropped to the floor and laid there crying. He ain't ever put a hand on me since."

Eddie's eyes welled up with tears. "I didn't want to hurt him like that, but I couldn't take any more of his beatings and his not loving me as a son. He was a mean father. Today, I feel sorry for him. First time in my life I ever felt sorry for anyone."

Using his shirtsleeve, Eddie wiped his eyes. "Sorry guys...don't mean to act like no little sissy. From that moment on, my father never spoke to me or bothered me again. I was only fourteen years old. It was now up to me to take care of me, and I had just learned lesson number one: Fear rules. I used fear to keep people from hurting me and fear to keep people from ever getting to know me. I was always afraid that if you ever got to know the real me, you would find that I was afraid on the inside, and then you would hurt me.

"All my life I've lived with this fear, never trusting anyone and always looking for an excuse to hurt someone so that you would know not to mess with me. I've never been able to trust anyone. What I would have given for just one true friend.

"I had no one to talk to, no one to share the dream I had about someday becoming rich and famous. Who would have believed me? Who would ever have loved me?"

Looking up at the ceiling in an attempt to stem the tears that were now flowing, Eddie added, "Like many of you, I was all alone and scared. Then one day someone had the courage, the nerve...."

He stopped and smiled down at me.

"...to stand up to me. Can you imagine that some punk by the name of Jim actually took me on? He dared get up in *my* face and tell me that I was not God almighty, that what I did was wrong."

Pausing, Eddie looked around the room.

"You all know how I took that—right? I swore I'd kill him. I was so angry and so scared that anyone would ever pierce my armor of protection that I had to kill him before I wimped out and became just a regular man. I couldn't be no regular man—I was Eddie."

Eddie paused and laughed at himself. He looked over at his sister Carmen. Smiling, he blew her a kiss.

"Even Carmen turned against me. She fell in love with Jim—snuck off behind my back to see him. Then get this! She *threatened* my life if I hurt her precious Jim."

Stifled laughter and murmurs of shock rippled through the crowd.

"Finally she offered to die for him in his place: '**Kill me**,' she screamed in my face. 'If you have to kill somebody, kill me.' My little sister, who I was sworn to protect, talking to me like that—bet you didn't know that, did you, Jim?"

My eyes had been slowly filling up with tears as Eddie spoke, but now—I was shocked! Never could I have let her die in my place—never.

"When she said that, I remembered that Joey had once said that Jesus died for us. He took our place. I couldn't understand it then, but when she offered to die for Jim, I wanted to experience that kind of love. No one had ever loved me like that. *If Jesus and God are for real,* I thought to myself, *if this Christian love stuff is real, then I want to be loved like that. So I talked to Joey.*

"Boy did we talk; we talked 'til three in the morning before I finally said yes, yes I want God in my heart. Now, I am a changed man; truly changed. I can actually feel the love that God has for me.

"I experienced it like a fresh snowfall covering me with love and forgiveness. Oh yeah, that's the other part. I feel forgiven by God for all the bad that I did, and I went home and asked my dad for forgiveness—Mom too. I even asked Jim to forgive me, and Carmen too."

Eddie paused so that his next words had impact.

"Now you know why I didn't kill Jim. I couldn't kill Jim. He's my brother, and I love him."

Eddie walked over to me. I stood and gave him a big hug. We truly were brothers and soon would be brothers-in-law.

Eddie had agreed to be my best man at the wedding whenever Carmen and I got married. I was so proud of him.

CHAPTER 35

J oey walked up and hugged Eddie and then took the microphone and walked over to where Carmen was seated. She rose slowly. Being Eddie's little sister, she had always shunned any attention, but she was also really shy.

Taking the microphone in both hands, she held it very tightly. Instead of her faded jeans and cut off T-shirt, tonight she wore bright white pants and an equally bright white blouse.

"As you can see, I'm wearing white tonight," she said, "Because for the first time in my life, I feel really clean and brand new. For years, I felt unloved and unwanted. I always thought no one really wanted me—except for the boys who wanted my body. I was so desperate for love sometimes that if it had not been for fear of Eddie, I would have gladly given my body to anyone who would've shown me love. I'm sure some of you girls can relate to that."

Walking more toward the center of the room, Carmen said, "Guys are lucky. If they want to feel loved, they can just go out and find some girl—any girl. It doesn't matter to them. Sex makes them feel better about themselves. When we girls do the same thing, we are called hoes; it's not fair.

"Over the years, I've discovered that life isn't fair. Sometimes, I've been so lonely that I thought about jumping off the roof. But, I was already afraid of heights, and it was a seventeen-story drop to the ground...."

Carmen waited as a rustle of nervous laughter went through the crowd. "When I met Jim, I thought to myself, *Wow, now here's a really nice guy. But what would he have to do with me? I'm just a tramp—a tramp from the projects.*"

Her eyes moistened. She choked up. Looking up and took a deep breath. "I dreamed of the day when Jim would ask me out. I knew that it would probably never happen, but a girl can dream, can't she? More and more as time went on, I believed that just maybe it could happen. I saw the way he looked at me—you girls know what I'm talking about.

"I could tell there was some interest now. I plotted a time when I could see him without my brother finding out. I just had to see if I was right. Did he really care for me?"

She looked over at her brother as if still unsure of going any further with her story. He nodded a friendly nod that told her it was all right.

"Finally I asked a close friend to go and ask Jim to meet me. When we met, I told him that I loved him, and he told me that he loved me. We kissed, and I was on fire. I think that I would have made love to Jim right there, but we were warned that Eddie was coming our way, so we fled.

"I didn't see Jim for several days. Then it got crazy. Eddie went gunning for Jim, Jim fled somewhere...well, y'all know the rest. And then the most incredible thing happened. Eddie got Jesus, and there was such a big change in his life that it frightened me at first. I didn't know what to do.

"When he and Jim asked me if I wanted to be like Eddie—y' know, have Jesus in my life, I was too frightened. No way, I said—I needed time to think.

"When I finally realized that what made Jim so different from all the others was his love for Jesus and his strong belief that he was loved by God, I wanted to know more. The more I found out, the more I wanted to know.

"Finally, I just took the plunge. I asked Jesus to come into my heart. I don't know how it is for some of you, but for me and Eddie," she smiled in my direction, "the change was instant. I suddenly felt forgiven, clean, and loved."

Tears now flowed, and she made no attempt to stop them.

"It would make me so happy if each of you sitting here now would find this same happiness, especially my cousin Skamp. "Many of you think she is just a junkie ho, but she's more than that. She loves me and I love her. You don't know what a hard life she's had. Please don't judge her."

Carmen stood very still and silent for a few moments. Finally, Joey got up and hugged her, and took the microphone. Wiping back a few tears, he said, "Wow, what a night—hey?" Joey smiled at everyone. Carmen sat down.

"Anybody else want to share?" Joey laughed when the response was silence. After waiting for a moment, he said, "Then let's give a big Young Life cheer to Eddie and Carmen!"

The place erupted in applause. People jumped to their feet hooting and whistling.

I sat there stunned. We had just witnessed a miracle. The past two weeks in my life had been crazy. First my brush with death at the hands of Bennie, and then Eddie, and now this!

God, you sure are so good to me—so good to us all. I am so sorry that I ever doubted you. You are so good. "Well now," Joey said softly into the microphone, "you heard what God has done in their lives; how about you? Anyone else want to ask Jesus to come into their heart and give them this love and peace?"

He paused and looked around. Conscious of what a powerful moment this was and how it put so many on the spot, Joey said, "I'm going to ask you one more time as we quietly sing 'Amazing Grace'.

"As we sing, I want everyone to close your eyes. If you feel that you would like to talk to any of the staff, raise your hand while we sing. I'm the only one who'll be watching. Then we can get together afterward."

We closed by singing four verses of "Amazing Grace." Afterward, Joey gave each of us staff members the names of some of the kids who had raised their hands. Amazingly, Frankie was on my list—the same Frankie who had once said, "Mister, I can do it myself; I don't need God."

Wow! What an evening!

I gathered those on my list. There were three: Frankie, a guy named Sammy, and a girl named Sarah. We went outside and across the street where we could have some privacy.

Sitting on the steps of an apartment building, we talked for about an hour. Each said they wanted some time to think, and we planned to get together the next day at that same spot.

I walked back to the apartment with Frankie. He had a lot of questions. We talked for a couple of hours in our bedroom. Then I said good night, got undressed and jumped into my warm cozy bed.

There was so much to think about!

So much had happened—so fast.

Carmen, what a woman she is. Will I ever be worthy of her? She was the first person I'd ever felt really comfortable around. I didn't have to put on any act around her. She knew me and my faults, and loved me anyhow.

What a heart she had. I just knew she would help transform Skamp and some of the other girls. Many of the girls already looked up to her, but now, she would have a powerful testimony.

Well God, this has been an awesome time. What more could you possibly have in store for me? I drifted off to sleep.

CHAPTER 36

E ddie, you scumbucket…how is you doing?"

Without even turning around Eddie recognized the voice of the insult as belonging to Ricky, the man he had so brutally beaten just a month ago and run out of town. He was back.

If he was confronting Eddie, there was no doubt in Eddie's mind that Ricky's four brothers were with him.

Eddie and perhaps Carmen could be in for some really big danger—possibly a disaster.

What should he do? He had given his word to Joey that he would change his ways—no more fighting. But what about protecting Carmen?

Immediately, the night air exploded into a bright flash of white light coupled with enormous pain. Eddie had just been hit from behind by a baseball bat that Ricky had swung at him.

Carmen slumped against the wall. Her mind went blank.

Eddie pushed hard against the two guys holding him. He almost broke free.

All of a sudden, Eddie's mouth hurt something awful. He quickly realized that he had just been hit in the mouth.

He could feel pain from some broken teeth. His mouth filled with blood. He never saw what hit him.

Pain…so much pain…everywhere.

Oh, God, how could I have been so stupid? I should've never been traveling alone. Always travel with a couple of my boys. Traveling with Jesus now…He'll take care of me. Please Jesus, don't let them hurt Carmen—please.

"Hey, Eddie, wanna see something?" Ricky blurted out. "Watch this."

Eddie tried to look. One eye wouldn't open; it was swollen shut. The other opened only a little. It was enough to see the horror that unfolded.

Ricky pulled off his belt, wrapped the leather around his hand, and dangled the buckle. Swinging the buckle through the air a couple of times, he spun around and hit Carmen full force in the face.

"**EDDIE!**" Carmen screamed in pain. "**EDDIE!**"

Eddie struggled as hard as he could. Someone hit him again with the bat, this time on the knee. Eddie slumped down.

"Oh, no you don't, big brother, you're going to watch every moment of this." Ricky coughed. "You're going to watch everything we do to your sister."

Ricky turned toward Carmen and made a big show of pulling down his zipper.

"**EDDIE….**" Carmen cried pitifully.

"**EDDIE!**" she screamed at the top of her lungs

"**Eddie,**" she sobbed.

"**Stop!**" Carmen screamed.

Eddie fell forward into a brick wall and sagged to his knees.

Swoosh! The bat flew a second time.

This time it seemed much harder.

Blood flew from Eddie's head as he crashed to the ground.

He lay there lifeless.

"**Stop—for God's sake—stop!**" blubbered a hysterical and weeping Carmen.

"*Oh, stop!*" Ricky mocked in a shrill voice. "*Oh, please leave my big brother alone. Oh, please don't kill him.*" Ricky enjoyed mocking Carmen.

Kill him? Oh, God—NO! Please God…don't let these animals kill my brother—please, please, please. Make them stop!

Ricky's two brothers walked over to where Eddie lay and one of them kicked him hard. "**On your feet—loser.**" He fumed. "You're not getting off that easy." The two of them yanked Eddie to his feet and held him by the arms.

"**Ahh…!**" The scream escaped Eddie's lips before he could stop it. Never would he give these guys the satisfaction of knowing how bad the pain was.

Blood flowed down his head and onto his lips. The warm taste of blood infuriated him all the more. He was used to dishing out the pain, but he'd never had to endure it.

"*Oh, poor boy,*" Ricky baited. "*Did somebody hurt the poor boy?*"

Carmen struggled against the arms that pinned her to the wall. Ricky's other two brothers had her pinned tight. "**Stop it, you miserable cowards. It takes five of you to hurt my brother. He'll get you back. Whatever it takes, you'll pay.**"

"Think so, baby?" One of the brothers whispered in her ear. "Think so?" He laughed heartily. "*You just wait and see what we have in store for you. Heard you're a virgin. Not anymore—not after tonight.*"

A cold chill ran down Carmen's spine. ***Oh God, I never thought they might hurt me.***

PART TWO

CHAPTER 37

J im, WAKE UP."

Shaking me vigorously, Joey shouted, "**Wake up. Eddie and Carmen have been hurt**."

I had just dozed off and somehow fallen into a deep sleep.

Everything was so foggy.

What had Joey just said?

I could see that Joey had been crying. I came flying out of the bed and was on my feet immediately.

"**What? What did you say?**"

I tried to rub the sleepiness from my eyes and mind.

The fog, oh, the fog of my mind.

What was going on?

Eddie—hurt? That's like saying that the Empire State Building had just collapsed. This was something that just didn't happen.

Carmen? What about Carmen—and why the tears?

How badly was Eddie hurt?

Oh, God! What happened?

I looked around me and saw that many others were coming into my apartment. Frankie sat on my bed sobbing with his head in his hands.

All the others were crying too. *Please God—someone tell me what's going on.*

"*Sit down, Jim,*" Joey said.

Clarkie and Gee took my arms and guided me down to my bed.

"Eddie's been hurt pretty bad and may not make it. And, Jim, I don't know how to say this, but—**Carman's dead**."

Joey said it so softly, I almost missed it.

What was Joey saying? None of this made sense. Was I having a dream—a nightmare? Oh God! Please let his be a dream—a bad one. Please someone wake me up.

My eyes raced around the room looking for an answer...something to tell me that this was not happening.

Someone surely would tell me this was some kind of sick joke. Please!

Joey sat down beside me. "Jim, there's no way to break it to you nicely. We only found out a little while ago, and no one knew where you were."

I sat there dumbfounded. I had no understanding of what was going on. It felt like I was in a daze. As I looked around at all the people crying, it suddenly hit me.

From deep, deep, within arose a terrible pain and moan at the same time. "**No! No! No! No! No! Noooooooooo....**" I howled at the top of my voice.

Bolting upright, I raced for the door. Both Joey and Clarkie blocked my way.

Tears burst from my eyes. I stood there sobbing.

"**Please, somebody, talk to me.**"

"Jim, we don't have a lot of details just yet. Someone heard their screams and called the cops. By the time the police arrived, Carmen was dead.

"Eddie's in intensive care. Someone said they had seen Ricky and his brothers around earlier.

Ricky?

Why hadn't Eddie killed the SOB the first time?

No ...not my Carmen. Not my Carmen....

You promised me, God. You promised me...you promised me.

I sat there crying, my whole body trembling. Everyone was crying. I'd never seen so many people crying at the same time.

Everybody loved Carmen. Who would want to hurt her?—and why? Why?

Oh, God, please let this all be a really bad dream. I don't know what to do. Please, someone, tell me what to do.

What about Johnny? Carmen's mom? Skamp?

This just can't be happening—it just can't be.

Oh, God, I came here to save your children and to protect them from the evil one.

To love, not kill, but God, if Ricky did hurt Carmen—if she really is dead—then please, please let me kill him, please—slowly, excruciatingly, painfully—as painfully as possible.

Oh, God, what is happening to me?

I finally found the love of my life—my soul partner.

Please don't take her away from me.

If you do—I promise I'll turn killer. I'll kill everyone who is bad— just because.

"Jim." A warm strong arm pulled me into a nearby body. I wasn't even sure who it was. I just buried my head and cried.

Unexpectedly there was a really loud wailing.

Someone was crying at the top of his lungs, screaming something unintelligible—something horrible.

Someone filled with anguish.

An out-of-control shaking was overwhelming me. I shook and shook.

Suddenly, I realized that all that noise was coming from me.

I was the one screaming. I could not stop.

Help me, Lord. Help me—I'm drowning.

I'm going under, and I don't want to live. Take me home with my beloved Carmen.

I could not—no, would not let anyone comfort me. What did they really know about our love? How could they help me?

Carmen, oh my Carmen, it's all my fault. You should never have listened to me. Oh, that you ever looked at me. I wish I had been so ugly—just like I am now.

Why, Lord, why?

Why didn't you take me?

She was so needed here. How could you be so mean?

I collapsed onto my bed and cried. Back and forth I rocked, my arms clasping my body in the fetal position.

"Oh, God, no…God, no…God, no…."

I just lay there in a daze and rocked back and forth. Before I knew it, I had fallen sound asleep. I dreamed I saw Carmen; she was crying—no, screaming, *"Help me! Save me, Jim!"*

Suddenly I sat bolt upright. The room was dark and appeared to be empty.

Now's my chance. I'll sneak out, find Ricky and his brothers, and kill them.

CHAPTER 38

W here do you think you are going?" Growled John-John, as he leaped up from his bed and blocked the doorway, his hand quickly flicking on the light switch.

"**Move, John-John!**" I commanded, mustering all my strength and courage.

He was tough, but I had a lot of anger fueling me.

"I gotta go!" I glared at him knowing that I didn't stand a chance against him if he chose not to move.

I glanced behind me for any weapon that I might use against him to get him to move.

For the first time in the year that I had known John-John, I saw the fiery look in his eyes soften.

"Don't do it," he pleaded. "You can't change anything, and you can't bring her back."

"**He's gonna pay …they're all gonna pay.**"

Tears began to flow; I could not—did not want to stop them. "I really want them to suffer."

"I know you're hurting really bad. I can feel your pain, my friend."

"I gotta do it, John-John, I just gotta do it. The police aren't going to do anything about it; they don't care about people like us. Ricky and his boys have to pay—justice demands it …it's only fair."

"Yeah, I know, Jim."

"I mean …if only they had just insulted Eddie or Carmen, it would hurt me, but I could live with it. But what they did …they have to pay for it. They have to die—brutally. They cannot be allowed to escape."

" **I will kill them**."

I shouted loud enough for the whole world to hear. I could feel my face flush and begin to burn. I was nearly out of control, and I knew it.

I looked out one of the filthy windows at the rat-infested back alley. I knew that I was filled with anger and that nothing short of killing those brothers would satisfy me.

"Jim, listen to me, please. You *don't* want to go down that road. Once you do, there's no turning back. Everybody gets hurt."

I knew that killing or murder or whatever you wanted to call it was a sin, but this time it was different. This was justifiable homicide—revenge.

This was not a sin.

It would be the same kind of killing that God did.

God killed his enemies when he was angry with them; he even killed them when they disobeyed him.

And if revenge killing was a sin, so what? Who cares?

God will forgive me—he always does.

Without any warning, John-John shifted his stance. Stepping back and to the side, he said, "You're right, Jim; they need to pay. But you can't do it alone. I'll go with you."

Walking back into the bedroom, he knelt down and took a hold of his heavy footlocker. It was an old US Army surplus footlocker, still painted the awful color called olive drab.

Lifting it up, he gently set it on his bunk bed. Rolling it over onto its side, the bottom came into clear view. It was covered with a heavy towel that had been taped in place.

Pausing for a second, he sighed and then peeled back the tape holding the towel in place. Now I could see what was under the towel. Two .45 automatics were taped to the bottom. Alongside each was a clip of bullets.

Looking up at me, he said, "Once we leave here, there's no turning back. We either die in a gun battle with these guys or we spend the rest of our lives running from the law."

Delicately he removed the two guns and set them aside. Next, he removed the clips and with a loud click inserted them into the guns.

I knew the rule of using guns in a fight. You don't bring a gun to a fight unless you intend to kill with it or be killed by it.

My rage knew no control; these guys would die. Everyone would know by morning that I had exacted revenge for Carmen.

John-John put the footlocker back in place, tucked one gun into his belt, and handed me the other one.

"Well, Jim, let's do it. Let's kick butt—friend."

Friend—he called me friend.

He rarely spoke…and he never called me friend.

Was I doing the right thing?

Was I about to destroy the life of my new friend?

Something was troubling me.

Didn't Jesus say something about it being rare that a man would die for his friend?

Yeah, that was it.

And something else.

God died for us while we were his enemies.

Oh, God, I'm so confused.

It was time to act!

The time for thinking was past.

Still it bothered me.

Friend…he called me friend.

What right did I have to ask him to die for me?

Jesus died for me.

Now I was asking my new friend to possibly die for me.

Did my actions also cause Carmen to die?

God, am I responsible for her death also?

They might not have died if Eddie hadn't become a Christian.

I sank down into my bed, rolled onto my back, and just cried. I no longer knew what to do. My mind was so confused. I no longer could distinguish right from wrong.

It seemed like I was floating away into space—*away.*

CHAPTER 39

When I awoke, John-John was gone. I bolted upright and ran for the door. If he was going to die, I wanted to be there to die alongside him. Just as I reached the door, Joey walked into the room.

"Glad I found you, Jim. Eddie's awake now and can talk. He wants to see you." Eddie had been taken to Governor Hospital where he had remained unconscious since the attack until today.

I was torn.

What to do?

I couldn't abandon John-John.

Nor could I tell Joey about John-John's and my plan.

Oh, God! When will it ever end?

I unconsciously reached for the gun John-John had given me.

It was gone!

I raced down the hallway and out the door. What I saw next really shocked me.

Sitting on the steps, smoking a cigarette, was John-John.

I was so relived.

Then I wondered if Joey knew.

Oh, God

CHAPTER 40

The hospital was just a couple of blocks away. Only Joey and I were allowed into Eddie's room.

Eddie's head was bandaged and his leg was in a cast and propped in a sling hanging from the ceiling. His face was really messed up. His eyes were puffed shut. He could barely open them.

My heart broke, and I burst out crying. I just couldn't help myself. *Oh, Eddie, poor Eddie.*

Oh, my Carmen, so beautiful and so gone. My knees felt weak and my head started to spin. Quickly I grabbed the corner of his bed.

"**Ow!**" Eddie screamed. "**You punk, let go of my bed!**"

Tears streamed down my cheeks. "Eddie, I'm so sorry, so sorry." I stood there and just cried.

"Jim," Eddie said in a soft squeaky voice. "Jim, listen to me carefully. I know how much you loved my sister. You're a warrior, Jim, I know that—everybody knows that. Don't do it. I know in your heart you want to go and kill them, but don't do it, man. I can't let you die like that.

You're all I have now. Promise me…." He passed out. The nurse asked us to leave.

Joey and I walked in silence. Once outside the hospital, I started crying again. It was like a dam had burst. I was twenty-five years old, and I had never, ever cried. Now look at me.

"Let's walk down to your bench," Joey suggested. Again we continued in silence. It was a ten-block walk. I had a lot of time to think. I was glad I didn't get John-John killed. I was thankful that Eddie was alive. I missed Carmen something terrible.

When we reached the bench, Joey sat down. He said nothing.

I sank down to the bench and said, "Joey, I loved her so much.

"She's the only one I ever fully trusted. She knew me…knew what a goof I was and still loved me."

I stopped and just sat there and stared. The silence was strangely comforting.

"She loved you too, Jim.

"You made a difference in her world.

"You gave her life! You gave everyone down here hope. You've made a big difference. Don't destroy all the good you did with one act of hatred. Eddie begged me to tell you not to do it."

Joey looked at me for a long moment. "It's your decision. But this is reality."

He swept his hand around the neighborhood. "It was filled with violence before we got here and probably will be long after we're gone. The most we can hope to do is save a few. Some people would say that even God has abandoned these people. But, we know different, right Jim?"

I sat there for a long time and just listened.

"Eddie's gonna need you now more than ever. You know that, don't you?"

I didn't answer.

"It's gonna be real hard for him now. Everybody will be expecting him to kill the brothers. They'll see it as a weakness if he doesn't. But killing them won't bring her back, and it won't allow Eddie to share his new life in Jesus with anyone. He really wants to make a difference—now. He even said he FORGIVES them."

I felt so lost and confused. *Eddie forgives them? I can't. I will kill them.*

"You want me to help Eddie? Why? I'm such a loser. I've failed you and God over and over. I've nothing to offer—I'm just a sinner, a man who can't even protect my friends. Eddie may have forgiven them, but I can't."

I looked out at the stars, not that I could see any from here. They were just imaginary—just like all the other good things around here.

Joey got up from the bench. "The next step is up to you. Don't destroy all that I built either."

"Wait, Joey…there's something else I need to share with you."

CHAPTER 41

I paused a moment then blurted out, "**I've never felt loved before, not even by God. There—I said it! Now it's out—the truth!**"

Joey just stood there. He didn't scold me or put me down.

My secret was finally out.

"I did my best to love God, but I never really felt loved of God—only tolerated until he found someone better. I gave my life to Jesus almost ten years ago. I've tried my best to serve him, but it's always been a struggle. Problem is…I've never really known love from *anyone*. My mom and dad were real hard on me. Joey, I just wanted to be treated right by them. I had to stay out of their way—y' know—out of sight.

"When I gave my heart to Jesus, I felt wonderful.

"Then I learned that we are to call God Father, and even Dad.

"But I couldn't do that.

"Every time I tried to call God Father, it really hurt. I felt that God could love everyone else, but not me.

"When I was growing up, my dad was the local Boy Scout leader; all the boys loved him. He was so nice to all of them—except me.

"My mom, she always wanted me to become a priest when I grew up. So anytime she suspected that I might have done something wrong, even though I hadn't, she got angry at me.

"When I heard that God loved me, just as I was—I rushed into his arms.

"I was so desperate for love. But what my parents taught me kept coming back—that if anyone knew the *real* me, I would be punished again.

"God knew the real me, so He couldn't *really* love me. After all, he was my *Father.* Fathers don't really love—they just pretend.

"As I grew up, I began to believe what my folks taught me, that no one would ever really love me, especially if they knew the real me. Oh sure, I've had friends.

"Even my best friend in school, Ricky, betrayed me one day to a guy who wanted to beat me up. I barely escaped. Since then, I've trusted no one."

Joey sat back down and put his arm around me.

"Oh, yeah, then there was Stella; did I ever tell you about her?

"Don't tell me she hurt you too?" Raising his eyebrows in mock surprise Joey said. He didn't mean to be hurtful, but I was in no mood for it.

I ignored him. There was just so much pain. It seemed my whole life was a great big hole filled with pain. Trust—betrayal—pain; *God, is that really what my whole life has been about?*

"She humiliated me in front of the whole school. She ended up running off with some Puerto Rican. Strange that I should so love another Puerto Rican now. Carmen was the first and only person to show me real love, and the amazing thing is she knew something of who

I really was. Of course, she didn't know the me I'm telling you about now. But the guy she knew…she loved."

I stopped and took a deep breath. I rose slowly from the bench and shook my head.

"It's John-John that I can't understand. He and I have been roommates for a year, and he has rarely spoken to me. I always thought he didn't like me. Yet there he was, willing to die for me—even when we weren't friends. I just don't get it. People have said that they loved me—but he was willing to prove it—with his life. I just don't get it. Why would anyone love me like that?"

Once again, tears flowed freely down my face. I sobbed and sobbed. "I just don't understand. Why? Why would someone I hardly know die for me?"

"Jesus did," Joey answered softly. You've been through a lot, my friend, and you need some time to heal."

"Maybe I should just leave. Go somewhere else and start over."

"Not just yet," Joey said. "These kids need someone just like you. I'm sorry that you have suffered so much in life, my friend. But God has a way of preparing each of us for our roles in life. Little did you know when you read that book that brought you here that God had already chosen and prepared you.

"You see, you are just like these kids in so many ways, ways that not even I can match. Most of them have never known their fathers; they have only felt hatred for them. They were raised by their mamas, and they feel inferior. No man has ever really cared for them or shown them the kind of love and commitment that you've shown.

"Jim, you are God come down to these kids, to let them know that they are loved and are special in the eyes of God. You, my friend, are like Moses, come to set my people free. These kids need you."

"I don't know if I can ever be all that they need again. I loved Carmen so much."

"Jim, listen carefully. Everyone loved Carmen. These kids you are working with and even people you don't know have been watching you. Now, it is more important than ever that you show them how a Christian handles all that you've been through. How you live your life *now* will speak louder than all your words."

"Wow, Joey, I don't know what to do or how to act. What should I do?"

"Just be your goofy self…goof." With that Joey got up and left.

God, how do I forget what they did to her? I can't!

What do I do if I ever see them again?

CHAPTER 42

That night, Joey gathered his leaders together.

"Guys, we all know what Jim has been through.

"Jim, what you don't know is that this *is* the life these leaders you see here before you have witnessed time and time again in this violent neighborhood. Several of the fellows have lost brothers, sisters, and even parents in this violent neighborhood. We all have had to learn how to struggle with pain.

"When Jesus was being killed by his enemies, he asked God to forgive them."

Joey looked at me with a steady gaze. "Maybe you're thinking, *Yeah, but I'm not Jesus—I don't know if I could ever do that.*"

"You're so right. You could never do that. But you overlook that you now have God living in you. Someday God will make it possible for you—but not today. Today you get some rest. Allow God time to heal."

"Rest—heal—yes, I guess. It all seems so hopeless to me. We tell them about Jesus. We demonstrate the love and forgiveness of

God; some believe us and ask Jesus into their lives, but it doesn't stop the violence.

"Joey, we've become such a violent society bent on killing one another.

"The Bible says that God loves the whole world—everybody—but the Church isn't helping the world. We're not showing the love of God, and we're not stopping the violence that is destroying us.

"If God loves everybody, then how come he allows us to kill each other?

"How could he allow those pigs to do what they did to Carmen?

"It just doesn't make sense anymore.

"Carmen was so beautiful…so full of promise.

"Now she's dead, and those pigs are alive. It just doesn't make any sense."

I felt like somehow I was searching for answers that maybe weren't there.

"Why isn't the church open for people to come and pray and find God?

"Why don't the police patrol down here like they do uptown?

"Why is everyone here on drugs?

"Maybe drugs are the answer—maybe I should just get high and stay high?"

I sat back and folded my arms in a defiant stance.

"Maybe, we could let Frankie have the pleasure of taking you "cold turkey" for three days," Joey said, hoping to shock me into reality.

"I can't blame you for the way you're feeling right now. I think maybe your idea of leaving might be a good one after all."

"**What**?" It was different when I heard Joey say it.

"I want you to take some time off. Go back and visit your good friends in DC and then come back—if you want to.

"But if you come back—and I say if, that's up to you—you need to come back ready to go to work and help these kids."

He looked at me with warm and understanding eyes. His eyebrows rose as if to say, *do you understand?*

I smiled, and he smiled back

Bowing his head, he prayed, "Father, I ask you to heal Jim's troubled heart. All his life he has been afraid. All his life he has been lonely. He finally found the love he was so desperately searching for—and someone took it away.

"You know him and you know his heart.

"Help him, Jesus.

"He loves you so much and has given so much for you—even to the point of his life. You rescued him so many times. I know that you love him.

"Please help him to feel loved. Thank you for John-John demonstrating to Jim the kind of love you demonstrated to all of us on Calvary.

"Now take good care of my brother as he goes to DC. I pray, Lord, that he will come back. We need him here. But it has to be his decision, Lord. Amen."

Joey stood to his feet. "Good luck to you, Jim, whatever you decide to do."

"Joey…I don't know if I believe anymore."

"Believe?"

"In God."

CHAPTER 43

I lay in my bed for several days, barely eating anything. Occasionally Joey would bring me some cheeseburgers.

What could I do?

What should I do?

I just lay there and sobbed.

Carmen's funeral was scheduled for Sunday afternoon. After that, I would leave for DC and try to put my life back together again. Everyone just left me alone. Occasionally I would get up and go down to the deli to get something to eat.

Scott, the owner, was always nice to me. "Jim, I heard about what they did to Carmen. I want you to know how sorry I am. In my basement, I got some guns—lots of guns. I've got some friends too. If ever you want to go and kill them all, we'll help you.

"Scott, you've always been a good friend. Times when I was short on cash, you let me work for my meals. I really appreciated that." I laughed. "Feels good to laugh."

"Anytime you need someone to talk to, someone who's an adult and no punk kid strung out on drugs, I'm here for you."

"Thanks, Scott. You don't know how much that helps me right now—thanks."

I wandered back to my apartment and sank happily into my bed. It felt good to be alone.

God, if you're there…help me.

I hurt so much.

You knew how much I loved her and needed her. I gave my whole life to you.

Why? Why didn't you protect her?

Day after day, I just lay there. I couldn't pray any prayer other than *why?*

Life just didn't make sense anymore.

Eddie was still in the hospital. He was recovering—some. It had been four days now.

Who was really responsible? Ricky and his brothers?

Eddie?

Me?

You, God?

Oh, yeah, I know, you're not really responsible for anything bad. *You get all the credit for anything good, but something bad, well, that's Satan, sin, or me. Well, I loved her. I would never have let anything happen to her if I could have stopped it.*

Would she have been better off if she never gave her life to you or if she had never met me?

I wish I had some answers.

What did she do to deserve such a death?

What did I do to have you treat me so badly?

In the Bible, you only punish people for being bad. David was punished by you for being bad, yet you say in your word that you loved me. **Why don't you love me?**

My whole life I've been betrayed by those who are supposed to love me. Why?

What have I ever done to deserve so much hate from you?

Please—just take my life and let me die.

CHAPTER 44

Eddie came to the funeral. He walked in slowly, on crutches. The small chapel at St. Chris's, where Carmen had testified only ten days ago about her love for the Lord, now held her body in a casket. The church overflowed with people. She was deeply loved by so many.

I sat on a bench in the back.

Several people went up and paid their last respects to her.

I couldn't move.

In life, she had been so beautiful. I had never been to a funeral before—never even seen a dead person. What did she look like? I wanted to know—yet I was afraid to look.

Soft sounds invaded my heavy thoughts

"Amazing Grace...that saved a wretch like me. I once was lost, but now am found, was blind, but now I'm free."

I sat there and listened as they sang.

God, what do I do now?

I once was free *but now I'm a lost wretch—what do I do?*

What do I say to Eddie? I'm sure he thinks it's all my fault.

The singing stopped and a still hush fell over the entire place.

I sat there staring down at my feet.

Next to me sat Frankie and Caesar. They had each gone up to put a flower on Carmen's casket and say a prayer for her.

"She was a great gal."

I didn't have to look up to see who was speaking. Joey's voice was very familiar to me.

"In her short life, she didn't have much of a chance to do a whole lot. But the one thing that I can say for Carmen is that she was a big…a very big…lover.

"She loved her family and her friends.

"There wasn't anyone she wouldn't help. When we all turned our backs on her cousin Skamp, Carmen remained a loyal and loving friend to her.

"Jesus tells a few stories about women.

"In his day, women weren't prized very highly. But Jesus was different; he showed great love and respect for women. Had Carmen been living then, she would have been one of Jesus's favorites.

"In her last days here on earth, she finally found the love and peace she had been searching for. She found that in God.

"The last days of her life were filled with a new joy.

"An unrestrained joy.

"She really loved living.

"She really loved her brother Eddie with a newfound love, and she loved Jim with all of her heart.

"Why did God allow this terrible thing to happen to her—to all of us? I don't know. But He did, and she is finally in a safe place now."

Thoughts and memories flooded my mind as Joey spoke. I didn't hear much of what he said.

188 | JIM BOYD

A couple of others stood and said a few words about Carmen.

When Frankie got up to walk to the front to say something, I quickly used his absence as an opportunity to slide out of the pew and out the back door.

I needed more time to be alone.

Let the others bury Carmen—not me.

I wouldn't have anything to do with putting her in a hole in the ground—not me—no way.

Maybe, just maybe with everyone here at the funeral, no one would see me if I slipped back to my apartment, got John-John's guns, and went and killed Ricky and his brothers.

Yeah—just maybe I could get away with it. Then maybe I would kill myself and join my sweetheart.

Yeah, that's it—we can be together for eternity—tonight.

Thank you, Jesus—thank you.

CHAPTER 45

Racing back to my apartment, I quickly unlocked the door and dashed to John-John's footlocker. Heaving it up on his bed and rolling it over, I pulled back the towel.

GONE—they were gone.

Where did they go?

Why?

Oh, God, please don't cheat me out of this chance.

I put the towel back in place, lifted the locker from the floor, and left the apartment.

Now what?

I headed in the opposite direction of the church. I didn't want anyone to see me nor did I want to see anyone. I had to get away.

Where to? DC? Not tonight.

Then where?

Mindlessly, I headed for the subway. *I'll just get away.*

As I entered the doors of the subway, I smiled to myself. I had just walked six blocks to the subway, down two flights of stairs, paid my fare, and was now on the subway, and I didn't remember any part of the walk. There was a seat next to a sleeping drunk close to the door. Nobody would bother me there. I could stay on the train for days and nobody would bother me.

Oh, God, what do I do? Eddie's gonna need me. So's Frankie.

Can't just run out on Joey like this, can I?

Sure wish I knew you better, God. Sure wish I knew my Bible like Joey does.

"Great is Thy faithfulness...great is Thy faithfulness...." Hmm, strange time for that song to be playing in my mind. Pastor Dick used to close the evening services by singing that hymn.

I need to talk to him. He knows so much, and I know so little.

Feeling so overwhelmed. Don't know what I'll say to Eddie...it's my fault, I know.

If it weren't for me, she wouldn't be dead.

What will he say to me? How is he feeling? God, I never stopped to think about him. Been so wrapped up in my own world of pain—never stopped to ask him how he is feeling. Probably wishes he'd a-killed me, by now. Big mistake on his part that he hasn't already. Maybe he still will.

The train screeched to a grinding halt. Outside of the window, a big sign read 42nd Street.

This is the infamous 42nd Street stop...lots of movies upstairs...lots of XXX movies. Gosh, I'm twenty-five, and I never saw a XXX movie. I could stay there for hour's...maybe even days.

Slowly I made my way out of the train and up the stairs. A hot dog stand was nestled against the wall next to the stairs. The mouth-watering enticing aroma of freshly cooked hot dogs fought its way through my clouded mind. All thoughts of Carmen, me, or God were gone. The only thought was of consuming some hotdogs and a soda.

The old man at the hotdog stand just stood there reading a sports magazine. He seemed like he couldn't care less if I wanted to buy anything.

"I'll take two dogs with cheese and chili."

Without saying a word, and still holding his magazine in his left hand, he grabbed a rag with his right hand and carefully lifted the top of the pan the hotdogs were cooking in then delicately placed the lid on the cart, grabbed a tong, and fished out two red plump hot dogs.

The hot dogs had split apart and had a crack running down the center. Finally looking up at me, he closed the lid and grabbed two rolls from a nearby bag.

Putting his magazine down, he picked up a bottle of liquid cheese and filled the large crack in the hotdogs to overflowing. The cheese flowed onto the bun. Next, he dipped a large spoon in a tub of chili and drowned the whole bun and hotdogs. It truly was a work of art.

Handing me the two dogs, he then wiped his hands on his apron. "What kinda drink, mister?"

"Root beer, please."

"Three bucks."

I paid the man, walked over to the curb, sat down, and wolfed the dogs in a few bites. Oh man, they tasted so good. It had been days since I'd really eaten anything. Now here I sat on a curb on a busy street, and not just any street, but 42nd Street in New York City, eating a sloppy, dripping hot dog and washing it down with a fizzing root beer. For the first time in days, life tasted good again.

By the time I had finished the second hot dog, it had begun to rain. Suddenly it turned into a cloudburst with rain pouring down everywhere. Jumping up from the curb, I scrambled over to the closest shelter, a movie theater overhang. Looking up, I saw that I was standing in the doorway of a XXX movie theater. Smiling to myself,

I thought *wouldn't Pastor Tom be embarrassed to be seen standing here with me now?*

Arriving back at my apartment, I went straight to bed without undressing. In the morning, I would talk with Joey some more. For now, I was tired—real tired.

John-John was sound asleep. Neither Frankie nor Caesar was in their beds. I lay there waiting to go to sleep. Nothing was happening.

Just still silence.

Still I waited. What was happening? I was really tired, but nothing was happening.

CLACK—the sound of a key turning in the lock of my apartment caught my attention. The door opened and the light in the other room was turned on. Someone walked over to the doorway and stood there for a moment before closing our bedroom door. It was then that I heard the soft voices of Frankie and Caesar. They were talking about Eddie. I couldn't make out what they were saying, only that they were talking about Eddie.

"Eddie says that he wants no revenge killing against Ricky or his brothers," I heard Frankie say a little loudly.

"He changed," Caesar said in a muffled voice. "I hope it's for real; seems to really love Jesus."

"Oh, I think it's real. God is already working wonderful miracles through Eddie" was the last thing I heard anyone say before I fell asleep.

CHAPTER 46

The next morning I showered, dressed, and went to Joey's apartment.

I knocked on the doorframe of the open door. Joey was always up early, and he opened his door as soon as he finished his prayer time. Everyone knew that Joey was a real prayer warrior. Staff meeting wasn't for another hour.

"Come in," Joey said without looking up from his notes. As I entered, Joey rose quietly and gave me his now famous big smile. His smile always lit up his whole face.

"Welcome, Jim," he said as he hugged me real tight. For a long moment neither of us moved. We just hugged each other real tight. A lot of pain had happened to the both of us in the last couple of days.

"How you feeling?" Joey asked, returning to his seat.

"Want some coffee?" He got up and went to get me some coffee.

Returning with my coffee, he said, "So…." Joey took his seat and said nothing more.

"I don't know …I just don't know." I shrugged my shoulders. "I mean, why is God doing this to me? I just don't understand. I trusted him!" I could feel the emotions welling up inside of me.

I looked up at Joey and shouted, "**I _trusted_ him**! Jesus said he would give me the desires of my heart if I followed him, but he knew how much I loved Carmen. Why doesn't God love me anymore??"

The tears began to flow again.

Man I hate this. I'm a man—men don't cry. All I've been doing the last week is crying. I hate it!

It's just not fair… just not fair. I should hate God for this. Maybe in some ways I do. But Jesus is all I have left. I am a hopeless prisoner of God's. Without him, I am nothing. Nothing!

Joey sat there quietly. He just looked at me with understanding eyes and sometimes looked at the floor. I felt that Joey just wanted to give me plenty of time to speak. I wasn't even sure Joey had any answers, but I sure hoped so. I was so tired of hurting.

"Jim, I don't have all the answers, and I never will. I do believe that God is doing a special work in your heart and life and that for now, you're just gonna have to trust Him. I also believe that you need some more time to heal and grieve your loss. As I said before, why don't you take some time off and go back and see some of your good friends back in DC?"

"I guess maybe you're right. I can't change or undo anything here. I created this mess, and I need to find the answers.

I just don't know that I believe that God loves me anymore."

"I know…I …I know."

After a long pause, Joey said, "Let's pray."

I didn't hear much of what he said. I was so into my own thoughts. I just remember hearing him say amen.

Joey got up and went into the back and started making a fresh pot of coffee. Soon the rest of the team arrived, one by one. As each arrived, he patted me on the shoulder as if to silently say, *Jim, I'm here for you.* I said nothing. I just sat there numb.

You could always count on me to be the life of the party—full of jokes and wisecracks. Now I just sat there numb. Once again, I felt so out of place. Once again, I felt that someone who I had trusted with my very life had let me down—betrayed me.

Just like Stella and Jose.

Just like all the rest. **God, it hurt so much.**

Without saying a word to anyone, I quietly rose and walked out of the room, down the hallway, and outside. A blast of cold air reminded me it was now winter, and I had no winter clothes, not even a jacket. It didn't really matter, I felt so numb anyhow. Besides, I had my anger to keep me warm. I just started walking.

There was nothing left of me anymore—nothing.

From *winner* ... to nothing ... in just one year.

Where do I go from here?

"Guys we really need to pray for Jim. As you know, he is going through a very rough time in his life, the roughest ever. We all need to just show him a lot of love and support. No matter what crazy things Jim says or does, just give him some space for now, OK?" Joey looked with serious intent at each man and woman on the team.

They were an awesome team of dedicated volunteers. Most were from the area, and had grown up here and gone through the rough roads of drugs and gangs. At some point, each had given his or her life to Jesus, and now they were a dynamic part of this team. Now they were the local leaders who reached out to these kids every day.

"I'll keep an eye on him, Joey," Clarkie said. "I can feel his anger. Years ago, my father betrayed me to some drug dealers; it almost cost me my life. I know what it is to feel so lost and lonely."

"Good idea, Clarkie; why don't you and Li'l Eddie check on Eddie. Let me know how he's doing. Frankie, keep the gang informed on Jim and how he's doing." Joey sighed deeply.

"Guys, it's going to be a tough time for us all—the next couple of weeks. We're going to need a lot of prayer."

Joey then led everyone in prayer for all that was going on.

"OK, everyone, you know what to do—scram. I've got some phone calls to make."

Slowly they all rose and made their way outside.

Joey walked over to his desk, opened one of its drawers, and pulled out a small black book. Thumbing through the pages, he found the phone number he was looking for. Picking up the phone, he dialed the number listed.

"Phil Jordan? This is Joey Jones from Young Life in New York City, Jim's friend. I need to talk to you. Jim's in trouble and I need your help...."

CHAPTER 47

E ddie, man, I'm so sorry." I stood at the foot of his bed and looked at him with tears gushing from my eyes. *Tears again. When will they stop? When will this be over? When will I start acting like a man again?*

Eddie opened his eyes and looked at me. This was my first visit to him since he had returned to his apartment. I just couldn't bring myself to face him. He knew that I felt that all that had happened to him and Carmen was my fault, but I just didn't know if I could take it if Eddie blamed me. I just didn't know.

"Jim," Eddie said softly, "I know you been suffering a lot. Don't blame yourself, my man; it wasn't your fault. Fact is, if anyone's to blame, it's me. I know that, Jim. My little sister…." His voice broke and he cried softly. There was nothing but silence—hard unbearable silence. It was killing me.

I need to get out of here—New York City—life. I don't know where I'll go. Maybe Joey's right; maybe I should go back to DC and spend some time with my friends there.

How will I ever tell them? How could I explain what happened here? Most of them have never experienced this kind of violence. They've only read about it in the newspaper.

How would I get there? I have no money. My car's not running. Nothing's really working right in my life. God, I just can't believe this is happening. I gave it all up for you, and now you've taken it all away. Why? I just don't understand.

I snapped out of my self-pity and walked over to Eddie's bed. I put my hand on his shoulder. He was still crying quietly. "I'll be back, man, I'll be back," I said, "but I gotta go away for awhile. I don't know when, but I'll be back."

Quickly backing away, I turned and headed out the door before I cried again. *This is it. No more crying. It's over.*

Never again would anyone or anything cause me to make such a fool of myself. Real men didn't cry—period.

I walked as quickly as I could out of the building. Feeling that the elevators were too slow, I raced down the exit stairs taking them two at a time. I couldn't get away fast enough.

Once outside of the apartment house, I began to run. I ran faster than I had ever run before, with no idea where I was going.

"Hey, slow down, man, wait up."

It was Frankie. What was he doing here?

"Man," a huffing and puffing He came up to me.

He stopped real close and placed his hand on my shoulder. "Joey asked me to keep an eye on you, but…" he chuckled, gasping for breath, "I didn't expect to have to run a marathon."

"Sorry, Frankie."

"Jim, we all know you're hurting. We're hurting too. We're family. Don't shut us out. When you hurt, we all hurt. If it was one of us, you'd hurt for us. Come on man, come home with me." Walking closer he put his arm around me and hugged me tight.

We walked back to our apartment.

"I called Phil Jordan and talked to him," Joey said with sadness etched on his face. "They are expecting you. I took the liberty of buying you a train ticket. Everything's all set for you to go to DC, Jim. You need to go."

"Thanks, Joey, I know you're right. Just don't know what it'll solve, but I'll go. Fact is, I'm just so tired. I can't fight anymore. Went by Eddie's apartment to see how he's doing." I couldn't say another word. I felt the tears trying to come again, but this time there was no way I was going to let that happen. I was done crying. I was a man now.

I walked over to my favorite chair and just slumped down. Joey had a really comfortable recliner, and I loved it.

Joey said nothing for a few minutes. He just sat there.

Finally, he said, "Come on, Jim," and he rose from his chair and reached out his hand to help me out of mine "Let's get something to eat. Don't know about you, but I'm really hungry." Funny thing about Joey, when he wanted to comfort someone, he always suggested going out to eat. That man could eat too. He always ate a lot and never gained any weight.

We walked down to the corner deli, a favorite of ours, and slid into a booth near the back. Joey ordered two cheeseburgers and two cokes for us.

"I don't know what to say when I get back to DC. Everybody there knows me as this strong Christian leader—always smiling and cracking jokes. I've always had all the answers, but now, I feel as if I have none. They've always looked up to me. What will they think of the new me…a man with no answers…a former leader who no longer wants to lead?"

"I hear you, Jim. As you know, I'm on your side no matter what. You know that the whole team stands with you, don't you?"

I inhaled a deep breath and let it out slowly. "Yeah—I know. Thanks, Joey."

Leaning back against the booth, Joey continued slowly and quietly. "Jim, you don't have to be a great Christian leader anymore. Just be yourself. These kids know who you are. Just being there for them and being one of them is all God is calling you to do or be." Joey clasped his big hands behind his head and gave me his big smile. He sure was a warm and caring leader.

"I guess I'm just scared—afraid of how they'll perceive me after all these years of building up my persona as being a great, loving, and all-knowing man of God. I don't really know if I should go back there or just stay here and try to sort things out."

"Well," Joey said, and he quickly leaned across the table and stared directly into my eyes, "that's not an option. I'm in charge here, and I'm ordering you to leave! Go—go away to your friends. If they are the great friends you've always said they are, they'll understand and grieve with you."

He stared deep into my eyes as if he were looking into my very soul to see if I was getting his message.

PART THREE

CHAPTER 48

J im," Phil said as he hugged me hard. "Good to have you back. How was the train ride?"

Phil had driven from his work to the train station to pick me up.

"Peggy's got a good home-cooked meal waiting for us. Bet it's been a long time since you had a home-cooked meal, especially one of Peggy's."

I smiled. Peggy, Phil's wife, was always such a good cook.

It was good to be back—back in the nation's capital.

It had been almost two years, but it still felt like home—sort of.

Phil showed me such love, and I needed that, especially now. He and Peggy were my spiritual adopted parents. They meant a lot to me. Had he rejected or questioned me at this point, I don't think I could have handled it very well.

Driving past the White House, Phil chatted constantly about all that had been happening in his life since I'd been gone. It was good to listen to him. I sat there captivated.

Phil led a Bible study at the Treasury Building and one at the Department of Justice. He was on a first-name basis with the vice president of the United States as well as with many senators in Congress. Phil was a "heavy hitter" in the eyes of many in Washington, DC.

That he should drop what he was doing to pick me up and take me to his home and treat me like a son meant a lot to me. In many ways, he was my hero. That could be a big problem, though; how to tell this giant of a spiritual leader that I was having doubts about myself *and* about God?

How would he handle it?

I listened halfheartedly as he spoke of all the wonderful things God was doing in the nation's capital.

After an hour's drive, we arrived at his big home in Bethesda, Maryland, on the outskirts of DC. Peggy greeted me at the door with a big squashing hug and a kiss on the cheek. "Welcome home, Jim," she said warmly.

Phil had invited the whole gang over. Many of them were home from college on vacation.

It was good to see Tuck and Denise and "Rev" Fred Harrison. This should have been a time of rejoicing, but that wasn't what was going to happen.

"So, Jim," Phil said, "how is it going? Joey says you are doing fine and that you are working with some pretty bad dudes. Ever get scared?

"Does water run downhill?" I laughed. "Yeah, sometimes it can get pretty scary."

Tuck leaned forward to catch every word. "What's one of the scariest things that have happened to you?"

Looking around, and then speaking very softly, I said, "after months and months of putting up with teasing remarks from Eddie this gang leader and at times being made a fool out of for his enjoyment, which I did to develop a friendship with him and be able to eventually tell them about Jesus, one day Eddy did something very wrong and it was going to cost me a lot of money and Joey his reputation; I just exploded at Eddie and told him off."

"Wow!" Tuck said with a deep slow sigh, what happened next?"

"Well, as I walked away, I realized just what a foolish thing I had just done.

"When I got back to the apartment, Joey had already heard that Eddie was gunning for me. Intended to kill me."

"Oh, my God, Denise softy exclaimed, oh my God."

"Yeah, 18 months of building a relationship with this gang and its leader Eddie who everyone knew was not only violent but, crazy and to make matters worse, I was in love with his sister. Now all that was gone!"

"Well, I struggled and struggled whether or not to run away and come back here and never tell a soul. But if I did, then both me and the Gospel that Jesus loves all of us and will protect us from danger would be a lie."

"So, what did you do?" Tuck asked.

"I'll tell you the 'rest of the story' after I rest up."

Denise smiled. "Well, that calls for a prayer of thanksgiving."

Everyone stood and formed a circle around me and thanked God for my deliverance. Soon the party broke up, and I went to bed. I had a long day planned for tomorrow and some bad news for Phil.

CHAPTER 49

The Jordan's lived in a spacious house with four bedrooms and three baths. My whole apartment, which I shared with three others, would fit into their smallest bedroom. Their daughter Dorothy was away at college, so I was able to use her bedroom. One bedroom belonged to their son Buzz, and the spare bedroom was Peggy's sewing room and an office for Phil. I never ventured into their master bedroom, but I knew it was big.

After dinner, Buzz went up to his room. Phil, Peggy, and I sat around the dining room table drinking coffee, eating dessert, and making small talk.

"Jim," Phil said slowly in his Georgia Southern drawl, "We love you, son. Now tell us what happened and why you're here."

I wished Peggy would leave and let us talk man to man, but I knew she loved me very much and wasn't going anywhere. How should I start? Where should I start? Did I dare tell them that in spite of all the love they have shown me over the last several years I had never really felt loved and accepted as just me? I was somebody in that town. Many people knew me or thought they knew me. Now it was time for the real me to be revealed.

There had been a time when I had lain on their couch thrashing about in pain. My back was so full of pain that I couldn't sit up. Phil had simply knelt beside me and prayed for me. Instantly, the pain was gone, and I was able to sit up straight. How could I tell a man with that level of faith that I no longer believed in God or God's mercy?

"Joey told me that someone you dearly loved was brutally raped and murdered—we're so sorry, Jim."

Now it was out. I was glad I didn't have to tell the whole story. I just had to deal with the pain.

I just sat there trying to figure how to start.

"Oh, Jim," Peggy cried. "I didn't know until just now." I started to cry too.

Stop it, just—stop! I will not cry. I am a man. God, if you're still there, and if you still have any feelings for me, then I beg of you, please, please keep me from crying like a baby.

I took a slow deep breath and tried to speak, but nothing came out. Nothing!

I surprised myself. Never did I expect something like this to happen. I noticed that my throat felt extremely tight. As I tried again to speak, a small hoarse whisper escaped from my mouth. I sat there stunned.

"It's OK, Jim," Phil said quietly while looking at me over his glasses, which had slid down on his nose. "It's OK. We'll talk later."

Peggy left the table in tears. I felt so bad for her. I was all my fault. Up until a few moments ago, she had been filled with laughter and was having a good time. Now, I had brought pain to her. What a sorry chump I was. So many times Eddie had called me that in fun, but now it was true. I was a sorry chump. So many other families had lost children to this crazy violence, and they didn't carry on like I did—or if they did,

I didn't know it. I wondered how the God that Phil and Peggy loved so much could do something like this to me. I loved God too!

God moved mountains in the Bible. He was always there to protect His people. Why hadn't he protected Carmen?

Oh, God, I'm sinking into a deep pit of despair. Help me or I'll ruin life for Peggy and Phil.

Phil got up and left the room. I sat there not sure what to do next. He had gone off to comfort Peggy. Would he come back in a few minutes? Should I just go to bed and talk with him tomorrow?

Why did I come here?

Why did I have to spoil such a lovely dinner?

Would I be able to get any sleep tonight if we did not talk?

Could I be able to get any sleep if we did talk?

If I told them of my doubts, would they remain as loving, or would they ask me to leave?

What kind of mess had I created for myself?

If only I had some money, I could catch a train back tonight. But working as a volunteer, I rarely had any money.

I decided to wait for an hour to see if Phil came back. Twenty minutes later, I heard footsteps coming down the stairs.

"What happened, Jim?" Buzz appeared in the doorway. "Mom's upstairs crying and Dad's in a bad mood. What did you do?"

CHAPTER 50

After spending a restless night tossing and turning with little sleep and thoughts of just running away, I decided it was time to face the music. I could hear people talking downstairs. Time to face my friends—my family—with the bad news.

The sad look on Peggy's face and the unhappy look on Phil's face told me that Joey must have told them that I was having a major struggle with my faith in God.

Phil and Peggy were from the deep Bible Belt of Georgia where one did not question one's faith or anything concerning God. I was facing a major Disaster with a capital D. These were some of my closest friends, but questioning one's faith was so alien to them as to be right up there with committing the worst kind of sin.

I remembered that when I was growing up, to drop the Bible on the floor was a tremendous sin. Allowing dust to collect on the family Bible, which lay on the coffee table, was to incur the wrath of my mom. All this was in a family that was not active in the church. Multiply that by the fact that the Jordan's took their faith extremely seriously, and I was in trouble.

The really sad thing was that until two weeks ago, I was just like them. I had taken my faith and my relationship with Jesus so seriously that I had given up everything to follow him and move to New York. Now I was possibly a bad guy. I didn't ask for this tragedy to happen to me. I didn't ask to have my whole world suddenly implode on me. Right now, I needed Phil and Peggy more than ever. This was the reason I had come back home. *Please, God, don't let them abandon me now.*

"Good morning, Jim," Phil said without looking up from his paper as I walked into the kitchen. Peggy sat there motionless and with a blank stare. Finally, after a moment or two, Phil folded his paper and cast it aside. The kitchen was a large room with three big windows that allowed the bright sunshine to flood in, which certainly seemed in contrast to the gloom that was present. A large table with six chairs around it sat in the center. The smell of fresh toast and bacon filled the air. Peggy rose from the table and walked to the stove. Without looking at me, she asked, "How would you like your eggs, Jim?"

Phil wore bifocals that he kept near the end of his nose. "Jim, Peggy and I spent half the night crying and half the night praying for you. We didn't get much sleep. Our hearts are broken for you."

Without any warning, I burst into tears—those stupid tears again.

Peggy turned around, eyes flowing with tears, and rushed over and hugged me so tight she squeezed the breath out of me. She just held me tight as she cried and cried. "Love you, Son," was all she could mumble. Thank God, Phil wasn't crying. Someday I was going to be a real man like Phil.

"Sit down, Jim," Phil said softly. "Son, it sounds as if you've been through horrible things up there. Tell us about it."

While I told them of the events of the last two weeks, Peggy cooked me up some bacon, eggs, and toast, which I feasted on. I hadn't had such good home cooking for years.

When I was finished, Phil asked us to join hands, and they prayed for me. They prayed that my broken heart would be mended.

Peggy then left the room, and Phil and I talked. "Jim, what happened to you—well, it just wasn't fair. You're a good man. You deserve better. I don't know why God has allowed you to suffer so much. I just don't know. Some things just happen that we don't understand, but we have to trust God. After all, God knows best."

When I heard these words, I seethed inwardly. My anger mixed with guilt was tearing me apart. I could not accept that a good God, who I had given up everything for, would treat me so. Yet, I loved Phil and did not want to crush him.

Oh, God, help me! I pleaded. *What do I do? What do I say?*

"I've arranged for you to meet with Dick (Pastor Halverson) later on this afternoon," Phil intoned sympathetically. He sat in his overstuffed leather recliner. I knew it was his favorite chair. We had had some long talks here while he drank his cup of coffee. Peggy always kept a fresh pot of coffee on the warmer.

"Thanks, Phil, I was hoping for a chance to talk with Dick. He always had so much wisdom for me. I rode with him once while he was making a hospital visit and used the time to ask a lot of questions I was struggling with."

Pastor Halverson, or Dick, as we all called him by his nickname, was a good man and a skilled counselor. I knew I could depend on him hearing me out.

We had had several small talks over the past four years. He was a friend I knew I could count on.

Phil continued to assure me that God did not make any mistakes and that this tragedy must have been Carmen's time to die. Everything he said only made me feel sadder and lonelier than I had for the last couple of days.

I had no way of anticipating what actually would happen when we met. It was a big surprise! It caused me to really think deeply. Now I was even more confused.

I sure hoped that Pastor Dick had some better answers. I was not sure how much more pain I could bear. To go from the valley to the mountaintop as I had for the past two years and then come tumbling down, faster and faster until I was completely out of control, hurt beyond belief.

CHAPTER 51

J im, come on in." A warm and friendly hand shook mine vigorously. Putting his arm around my shoulder, Pastor Dick led me into his huge office filled with a vast array of books. The entire office, all four walls, was filled with bookcases. Each bookcase contained different sets of books, usually a different color for each set. His desk was massive. Pictures of him and the president of the United States hung on his wall in a large open space in the middle of one of the bookcases.

It was no simple task to get an appointment with this man. In the past, I had to call his secretary and make an appointment weeks in advance. I was so lucky that he and Phil were such good friends. The top two corners of his desk were filled with wire baskets that contained several files each. The center of his desk was cluttered with piles of paper. Closing the door to his office, Pastor Dick led me to a corner where a couch and two chairs sat. I took a seat on the couch and he took one of the chairs.

"Tell me what's troubling you, Jim, and how I can help."

I told Pastor Dick about all that had happened to me the past couple of weeks and how I was feeling. "Dick, you know that I love Phil and Peggy and would never do anything to hurt them, if I could help it."

He nodded his head. "Sure."

"Phil was telling me that I've got to accept my tragedy as coming from the Lord. You know, like it was God's timing—as if God sent Ricky and his brothers to do God's work. Also, he told me that no bad thing can happen to us unless God permits it. I just cannot believe that the God I have loved and served is so cruel and heartless. I don't want to offend Phil and Peggy, but I just cannot buy into that crap. I don't know what to do or say."

Pastor Dick just sat there and looked at me with soft blue eyes, which somehow conveyed to me that I was safe. I could tell him the rest of the story. He was about fifty years old and had some weight on him. He stood about five feet ten inches, and sometimes looked like Santa Claus.

"Well, the rest of the story is that I don't know if I believe in God anymore." I held my breath waited for the firestorm that was sure to follow. What would this great man of God say now?

"Jim, I've know you for a while now, and I've watched you. You are a good man with a deep heart for God. You've had a rough life, and in many ways, you are just like the kids you're working with. They're treated as rejects by our society—throwaways who are brought into this world and then rejected by those who should love them the most—their parents. This world is full of children whose parents don't show them any love.

"In some ways, we're all like that, raised by parents who are still struggling so hard to make sense out of life that they don't have time to learn how to love and respect their own children. The church is responsible for much of the pain our children suffer. We put such high standards on how Christians should live their lives and raise their children that there is no time left over to learn how to be good parents.

"Your parents probably tried hard to do what was right, but they just didn't know how. They probably didn't have good role models themselves—right?"

"Yeah, you're right. Neither my mom nor my dad had loving parents. I've heard Mom talk about them sometimes. They treated her really mean. Dad's too. I never thought about it that way."

"I understand, Jim. So you spent your *whole life* looking for someone to love you unconditionally, just like a child would expect from his parents. Yet at the same time, somewhere along the way, someone you trusted let you down—maybe even betrayed you. I could see the signs when you were here: you were open and loving to all, yet at the same time closed to a real relationship.

"Somehow, we, the church, have taught that all that was really most important was our relationship to Jesus. Lost lonely people came to church, found a God who loved them, and then spent their lives trying to follow the church's teaching in order to earn Gods love and understand God. There was no time left for being a good person whose life was dedicated to loving others.

"I've seen it so many times. A young person comes to know Jesus and then throws himself into working for the church and loving everybody, afraid that someone might discover that he is not all that he is pretending to be. He builds a false persona and tries to become what he thinks he should be; he develops a protective shell.

"He becomes afraid that if anyone finds out who he really is, they will reject him. Then he *really* becomes a loser.

"Leaving his other friends behind and exchanging them for new church friends, only to be rejected by his new friends and church family, would be too much too bear, so he hides from the world and hides from his new friends. Sometimes we're all a bit like that. Unable to trust anyone, we don't let people get too close to us. But it is such a lonely life. It becomes just Jesus and me. I end up expecting God to do everything I ask him. I expect the world and God to serve me because I have given so much to them.

"In reality, neither God nor the world is able to fully satisfy our deep needs."

I heard what he was saying, and I knew he was talking about me. Thank God, I didn't cry. Some of the things he said hurt very deeply, but the way he said it made sense, and I understood.

"That's been me. You may remember that when I arrived here two years ago, I was working with Jerry Black in his ministry. Well, they believe in only giving your all to Jesus, nothing less. Everything else was only a distraction.

"The way I was trained was that if I was working with some Christians and they would not give me all that I requested of them, then I was to dump them—move on and find someone else.

"The thing that really messed me up was their belief that God sidelines or benches men of God who either displease him or don't give their all to the ministry.

"They cite King David and Samson as examples of great men of God who God later sidelined to the bench of life. I never wanted to be benched by God, so I gave my all, all the time and I was always afraid that if anyone ever found out that I was not giving my all, I would be benched by them as well as God. That would be just too much.

"I finally found in Carmen all the unconditional love God promised and my parents could never fulfill. Then God took it all away."

"That must have really hurt," Dick said.

"More than you know—more than you'll ever know." I paused and added, "Thank you, Pastor Dick, for your time and wisdom."

"Jim, I want you to know for sure that ONLY God can give you that love you are seeking."

~

I walked into the empty dark church and sat in one of the pews. I needed time to think, time to process all that Pastor Dick had told me. *Somewhere in what he said was the key to the door that would end all my pain and give me life.*

For the first time, I understood a lot about my life. Things made sense to me. My whole life had been about serving God by pleasing others.

How then do you serve God?

How do you show God that you love him?

Carmen loved God, and she loved her cousin. Wasn't that Carmen showing the love of God?

The only way that I had been taught was by pleasing key people and following their rules.

Rules, rules, rules. The great God of love and mercy could only be served by following so many rules. Rules that no matter how much or how many, I would always be in the place where Jesus said, "Even if you keep all the rules, and yet somehow break even just one, you are guilty of having broken them all."

What then was this thing called grace?

I was so lost.

I was all about trying to please everyone and winning everyone's love and respect while being fearful of people finding out that I wasn't perfect and rejecting me. Life was such an exhausting never ending battle for me.

I realized that somehow the church had taught me that I needed to be perfect. It wasn't enough just to be me. "Be ye perfect, as your Father in Heaven is perfect" was a verse in the Bible that somehow had been pounded into me.

I believed it. I made this such a strong part of my life. So, knowing that I wasn't perfect, I held others at a distance. Didn't want them getting close enough to find out I wasn't perfect.

No! Couldn't have that!

What a bummer! Serving the God of love had become a chore, a lonely, lonely chore. Hey, if I let others into my life too closely, I might become just like them—failures in need of rescuing—sinners! Wow! I really had messed up my life.

I walked slowly back into Dick's office.

Dick continued. "The heartbreak of all this is that one of the reasons Jesus died for us was to set us free from all the laws that the Jews had established to run their lives.

"God's message has always been the same: Love God and love your neighbor. Over the years, we church leaders have made up so many rules of how to live a life that pleases God that it suffocates us. We end up being miserable instead of happy.

"We tell our young people it is a sin to dance, drink, or smoke tobacco, or even go to the movies, even though some of us adults do it. Now, I'm not saying it is right to smoke; it's just not a sin.

"We adults have made everything that seems fun to young people a sin. Then these young people grow up to become guilt-ridden adults. They spend their whole lives trying to please God by living up to other people rules rather than knowing the Bible for themselves.

"Christians can sometimes become very arrogant, especially us pastors. Sometimes we demand our people do exactly what we say, even when we don't know why it is so important, and we don't do it ourselves. We see ourselves not so much in a battle against Satan as against each other.

"We fight among ourselves over whose church is the best or the right one or sometimes the only one. Why, just two years ago, I was at a conference where I met a pastor who told me in an angry tone that if I was not a member of *his* denomination, I was not a Christian and needed to repent.

"What stupid arrogance! The sad fact is that he did not know his Bible very well. He only knew what others told him to be true.

"That's where you are, Jim: trying **so *hard* to please God** and to show your love for God by setting a good example of what others have told you a Christian's life should be. When all along you have been totally missing the real reason Jesus died, he died to give you a life of love freedom and Grace . . . continuous forgiveness

"I'm so sorry that you've had to go through this all alone. It must have been really tough." Grace is perhaps the hardest to understand and accept concept of the church. Grace means that God knows we are human and doesn't expect ut to be perfect, just to be His friend and help others to become friends with God. God does the "saving" and the changing of our lives.

I let out a deep sigh and slumped back in my chair. "If only I had known, if only ..."

"Maybe it would help you a lot to know your Bible better. Maybe going to a Bible school would help."

"I don't know. You've given me so much to think about. You're right, I have been a slave to other people expectations—even those of the guys on the street. I try to live up to their expectations of what they think a Christian should live like. I've been so frustrated and lonely."

I got up off the couch and walked over to a window and just stared out. I needed time to think, time to process all that he was saying. He was totally different from what I had expected; I had so much to think about. Some of my thoughts were so contrary to what I had always believed. How could this be so? How could I have been so wrong? Or was he wrong?

No, it couldn't be that he was wrong; he was the expert.

This is all so amazing! I wonder if Joey already knows all of this. Maybe he's been trying to tell me, but I just wasn't listening.

Through the window, I could see some deer stepping tentatively out from the trees to cross the snow-covered field adjacent to the church. It was a perfect scene. The world was suddenly safe.

It's okay now, Carmen. I can let you go. I know that you are with Jesus and that God still loves me. Guess it's time I got back to New York and my family there.

CHAPTER 52

Excited—yes, that was the word that described how I was feeling. The week in Washington, DC, had been refreshing. The long train ride home gave me ample time to reflect on all that I could remember. My visit there reminded me that I was loved and respected by friends there. I came back with renewed enthusiasm.

I lay on my bed waiting for the others to awaken. The time on my watch was 6:00 a.m. *nobody* got up before 7:30 around here. But here I was, wide awake and excited.

Lord Jesus, thank you for being there for me. You know that I love you. It's just that I was so scared when Carmen died. I thought she was the only one who really loved me. I still love her and know that she is with you. Thank you for allowing me to have a small part in her coming to know you.

Her last days here on earth were incredibly happy days. You knew that things like this could happen, so you brought us together so that she might be joined to you. Many people, even churches have rejected these kids—but you didn't. Thanks.

Thanks for changing my selfish heart. I've been such a jerk. Help me now to change and become a servant, a lover of these youth you've placed within my trust.

Thank you for being my friend.

I remembered the song "Love Like a River." Yes, that was it. Jesus's love for me, for everyone, was a fast-moving river erasing all of our sins and making us clean and whole once again.

I sat on the edge of my bed and looked at the others sleeping there. On the bottom bunk opposite me was John-John the fierce street warrior. In the bunk on top of me was Frankie, one of Joey's trainees from the community, and over John-John was Caesar.

What a motley crew we made. Each of these guys had shown me in so many ways that they loved me and accepted me as one of them. Yet I had failed to see it because I was so self-centered. *God, forgive me—guys, I hope you can forgive me too.*

Perhaps I'll just get a shower and go for a walk.

CHAPTER 53

L ook who the cat dragged in!" Joey stood laughing as I walked
into the staff meeting.

"Oh no," Frankie moaned. "I thought we had seen the last of
you, or at least I had hoped."

"In your dreams, Puerto Rican, in your dreams." Leaning over
and putting my face close to his, I smiled a fake smile and said, "Kid,
I am your worst nightmare." Everyone laughed. I was home and I was
loved. I had been missed. God, it was good to be home again with
my family.

After a few announcements, Joey turned to me. "Jim, why don't you
tell us what's been going on and why you're here this morning."

"Sure thing, Joey. First of all, I need your forgiveness. I've been
such a jerk—such a fool. I always thought of myself as better than
you guys." I looked at Frankie, John-John, and Caesar. "I thought
I was someone special in the eyes of God, more special than
anyone else."

I told them all about the struggles I had been going through, my trip to DC, and the things the Lord showed me about myself. I asked for forgiveness from each of them.

I confessed that I had been a jerk and was now ready to become a part of their team if they would let me. They all stood and welcomed me back.

Joey said, "Well now, we got a lot to talk about this morning. I want to challenge each of you to be the leader that God is calling you to be. We're going to need a stronger level of commitment from each of you.

"Jim's right about one thing: you all are special—special in the eyes of God, but also to me and to the people of this area where we live. God has called each of you to be an important part of this team. I need each of you to double up on your commitment to Jesus and Young Life.

"There's something else we need to talk about. It's about the value of being a team player. Jim, since you came here, you've been the lone ranger. You've not been a good team player. Everything has been about you and the gang you work with. No wonder you felt so unloved; you wouldn't let anyone inside of the wall that you built around you.

"You said just a little while ago that you've been acting and feeling like you were somehow better than the rest of us. Well, now is the time for you to join the team and become truly one of us. Become a member of what is going on here, and let us in. Let us be a part of what is going on with you and the Puerto Ricans.

"No man is an island, Jim. We all sink together or we swim together."

"It's swim together or sink together, Joey," Clarkie said, laughing good-naturedly. Then everyone laughed. We all needed a moment to recover from Joey's heavy talk.

"Yeah, right," Joey said with a big grin. "Let's move on. Jim, what I'm saying is we want you to be a part of the team. We don't want you ever feeling lost and lonely again. Capiche? Entendió?" Joey smiled as he rubbed my head.

"Things got hot here, Jim, while you were gone, and we almost had another turf war. I want everyone to stay on top of things and let me know at the first sign of trouble."

We all responded that he could count on us.

"Clarkie, please close us in prayer."

After prayer, Joey walked over to me and said, "I need to talk to you. You got another problem."

My heart stopped. I could feel the pit of my stomach tighten into a knot.

What now?

Was I in some sort of trouble?

Did he not want me back?

Putting his arm around my shoulder, he led me outside and down to the corner. When we got to the corner and thus out of earshot, Joey back against the wall and said, "Frankie got high while you were gone. He's back on drugs."

"I shouldn't have gone away," I mumbled.

"Jim, there's something you need to understand. Just as you discovered that you're not perfect, and yet the rest of us keep on loving you, Frankie's not perfect, but he's still a Christian, and most importantly, he's your friend. He needs you, Jim. Frankie really needs our help. He can't make it here. We need to send him to live somewhere else. I'm going to make some calls to other Young Life groups I know and see if I can send him somewhere.

"It will be tough on him going to a new place where he doesn't know anyone or have any friends yet. The good news is I talked to Frankie last night, and he's actually looking forward to relocating."

Frankie high again, and Joey wanted me to treat it causally as if it were something minor.

I almost got killed trying to help him go cold turkey, not to mention the beating I took. Just accept it, Joey said. I didn't know if I could *just accept it.*

Treat him the same as I would any of the other Christians? Just didn't make sense. But, hey, what did I know about life? I was just starting over. Joey was asking me to trust him and his judgment.

Boy was I confused.

Just when I thought that I had everything figured out or at least somewhat under control, boom—the bottom dropped out again.

I loved Frankie, but could I just ignore his drug habit and treat him as if it never happened?

Joey looked at me sternly. "You need to understand that just as we all struggle to become free from sin, Frankie is struggling every day to become free of his habit. It'll happen one of these days—trust me. But it will take time and several attempts. One of the biggest helps we can offer is to get him out of here, away from José and the others."

"**José.**" My breathing became deep and my arms tightened in anger at the mention of his name. I could feel the heat rising in me as my anger grew. "**José again. I'll…**"

"You'll do nothing," Joey interjected. "Can't have you causing another problem. I just couldn't take it Jim, if Bennie killed you this time. Maybe it's time you left, too, if you can't take it. Maybe you and Frankie should both go away."

I could feel the tears fighting to pour out of my eyes and drench my face. No way was I going to cry; that old sissy was gone. I had just gotten back; this was my family. Why was Joey trying to hurt me? Frankie had sinned, and now Joey thought that I should go home too?

I sat on the curb. Joey and I were still alone. He stood there looking at me with sadness in his eyes.

"Some think that if they were to die, it just might be better than what they live in, especially here," Joey said. "So you see, Jim, we need to show these kids just how much God loves them by loving them ourselves—before they change. This is the message of Young Life. Not rules, regulations or the Bible being thrown into their faces, but loving them just as they are and telling them that we are living in the greatest time in history. Jesus came preaching the love of God, forgiveness, and joy.

"The church started out preaching these things, but somewhere this message got lost. It wasn't long before the message of the church became convert or die. Then it became repent, convert, or spend eternity in a horrible place called hell.

"People were forced to choose between becoming a Christian or spending forever in a burning pit ruled by Satan.

"While some of that is true, the basic message of Jesus—that God is LOVE—became lost. We in Young Life believe that God loved the world so much that He made a tremendous sacrifice to show his love.

"We could never reach these kids with the love of God if our only message was repent or die and go to hell. Most of them think that they are already living in hell.

"That's where I believe that you got mixed up. You learned from some of your other friends, and some churches, that to be a Christian was *to fear* God and to follow rules designed to make you more acceptable to God—sound right?"

"I never thought of it that way, Joey. I guess I thought that, just like in the army, you please those in command above you by following their rules; so you please God by following his rules. I was so afraid for anyone to find out that I wasn't all I was supposed to be or pretending to be. I lived in fear of the day that someone would discover a crack in my armor. I desperately longed to be loved for just being myself, but I was so afraid to be myself. I always knew there was more to life than what I was experiencing, but I just couldn't quite put it together.

It's amazing; a new light is dawning in me. Life is finally starting to make sense.

"I readily followed the rules that the church taught would bring me the love and acceptance of God because I was so desperate for someone to love me—especially God.

But I still never felt loved!

"Couldn't feel loved because there were so many rules—just couldn't keep them all. This is incredible!"

My heart was beating fast, just like the day when I first asked Jesus to come into my life and fill me with the joy that these other kids in Young Life had. So it was there all along, buried somewhere deep in my subconscious that God loved me just as I was. All He was asking was that I abide (live my life) in Him and trust God to lead me and not myself.

I jumped to my feet. "Joey, I got so much more to share with these guys now. I feel like a free man again. Born again—yes, that's me—born from love, not from fear any longer."

Joey extended his hand and yanked me to my feet and hugged me real tight.

"Thanks, Joey." The tears started to flow again, and this time I did not try to stop them.

CHAPTER 54

I t had been a week since I'd returned, and since Joey and I had talked about Frankie's leaving and possibly my leaving too. I had done a lot of thinking. Maybe Joey was right. Maybe I could continue working with Young Life in another city and go to Bible college at the same time and get to know God better. I really needed to know my Bible better. How could I share a message or tell about a God that I did not know so well?

Slowly, I grew used to the fact that Frankie was still Frankie, my best friend. He really was trying hard to quit drugs, but it had such a deep pull on him.

I went uptown to a Bible bookstore and looked at magazines about Bible colleges. I really fell in love with Moody Bible Institute in Chicago. Ripping out an information card from one of Moody's magazines, I filled out the card and mailed it. What would I do if they accepted me? I didn't know. I didn't say anything to anyone about it.

Eddie soon was off his crutches, but still needed a cane to get around. This was the new Jesus Eddie, as some were calling him now. The fierceness that Eddie once pursued as an evil gang leader, he now pursued as a man captivated by the love of God.

It was funny and rewarding to see Eddie so loving and playful. He had lost none of the respect of his gang; in fact, he had gained much more respect even from people not in his gang.

He helped Joey with Joey's new program of getting parents involved in the school so their children would have a better chance to get a good education. Eddie nicknamed this new program The Carmen Project. He knew that was something Carmen would have loved to be involved in—had she lived.

I missed Carmen.

Somehow, seeing her as a sacrifice that had brought peace and love into this corner of the world, just as God had sacrificed his Son, brought me some peace and joy.

"Jim, come to my office." Joey's loud voice echoed throughout the entire apartment house. I had just gotten out of the shower. The shower curtain had long turned black from the mold and mildew. At first, it kinda gave me the creeps. Made me feel dirty, even though I had just showered, but now, I rarely noticed it.

Noting the sense of urgency in Joey's voice, I hurried to his office.

"What's this?" He handed me a letter from Moody Bible Institute.

I ripped it open.

"I've been accepted," I said.

Blood pounded through my heart, and my breath became shallow as I yelled at the top of my lungs, "I've been accepted to Moody!"

"Joey, to me Moody is the best of the best Bible schools. I'm going to learn about Jesus, and God, and His great love for us all. When I come back, I'll make you so proud of me."

Joey stood there smiling that famous smile of his that said to people, I really am happy for you. "You do it, buddy, and take Frankie with you—please."

I laughed. *Take Frankie with me? What would I do with Frankie? How would he live?*

Where was I going to get the money to go now that I'd been accepted? Wow!

"Joey…" Once again the tears started to flow. "I don't know what to say. I'm so excited that a school like Moody would accept someone like me, and I want to go, but I don't want to leave my friends here. Besides…" I shook my head as reality set in. "I got no money."

"Sounds like a personal problem to me." Joey laughed.

Later on that day, I wrote a letter to Moody and told them that I accepted their offer and was coming, but that I had no money. I didn't know how God was going to provide.

Somehow, God would provide; I just knew it. Me, a Bible college student, and not just any Bible college—Moody!

The next three weeks sped by quickly. I was so excited about going; Frankie was so excited about coming with me. In fact, he was so excited that the remained clean the entire time. The whole neighborhood seemed excited for us.

Still, as the time of our departure was drawing closer, there was no word on how we would get the money. I wrote Moody again and again and told them that I was coming but that I had no money. Did they have any scholarships?

A week later I got another letter from them saying they had no scholarships and that if I did not have the money—**DON'T COME**!

Talk about a shock. I was stunned. I was sure that God had opened a door for me to go. What would I do? Everybody, including Frankie, was so excited about us going.

God provided a way, and it really blew my mind.

"Jim." Once again Joey's booming voice filled the hallways. "Telephone."

Me? Telephone? I rarely got any calls here. I always used the pay phone to make my calls. Who would be calling me, and on Joey's private phone?

Racing down the stairs, taking them two at a time and bouncing off the wall, I jumped the remaining three stairs and sped into Joey's office.

Grabbing the phone receiver from the desk, I answered out of breath, "Hello, Jim here."

"Jim," the soft voice of an old and dear friend said. My heart warmed when I heard his voice. So wonderful of him to call, but what did he want? "Dick Halverson here. How you doing, son?"

"Great! Just great…" was all I could get out. I was breathless from running so hard, and bewildered that such a busy and important man was calling me.

"You probably didn't know this, but I serve on the board of Moody Bible College. A request came through for us to pray for you. Said that you were committed to coming but had no money. Is this true?"

"Yes," I stammered, confused and slightly embarrassed.

"Well, I talked to the board at my church, and they have agreed to give you a full scholarship for as long as you want to attend."

I sank to the floor, falling on my knees and almost dropping the phone. I was stunned. What could I say? I just knelt there and stared at the phone receiver in my hand.

Rising from his chair, Joey rushed to my side.

"You all right? Bad news? Is everyone OK?"

"I'm OK—I think. Just can't believe what I'm hearing."

Putting the phone receiver back to my ear, I said, "Dick...I don't know what to say. I'm stunned. I'm bowled over by your offer. Why would they do this for me?"

"Why not? You are a man of God and you need help. That's what we're here for, and you're my *friend*—and that's what friends do for each other."

In my mind, I could hear Pastor Dick softly singing, "Great is thy faithfulness, O God my Father....Morning by morning new mercies I see. All I have needed thy hand hath provided...."

PART FOUR

CHAPTER 55

After hearing the good news Dick Halverson had shared with me on the phone, Joey called a special staff meeting for the next day.

Everybody came to the meeting. Even Michael brought some of his people from uptown, including Alecia and some of the other girls, to find out what was so important.

When Joey and I had finished sharing about all that had happened over the past several weeks and all the great things God was about to do, Frankie cleared his throat and stood up.

Frankie stood about five feet seven and was very skinny, like most drug addicts. He had dark wavy hair, which he combed constantly. "Mr. Cool" was his nickname. He actually was quite handsome.

Rising from his chair, he paced around for a moment or two.

"You guys know I ain't ever been more than a few blocks from my home here in my entire life. Moving all the way to Chicago with Jim is scary. Moving anywhere with Jim would be scary enough, but

Chicago? Only safe thing there is that Vinny lives near Chicago."
Everyone chuckled.

"Don't get me wrong, Jim's an okay guy, but well ...y' know."
Frankie shrugged his shoulders, reached into his pocket, and pulled out
his comb. Slowly stroking his comb through his hair, he smiled. "But, y'
know, Jim's no Mr. Cool."

At this, everybody roared with laughter.

Joey stood and held up his hand until everyone was quiet. Frankie
sat back down. "Well, on Wednesday night, we are going to have a
special club meeting at St. Chris's to say farewell to Jim and Frankie. We
want to send them off with a party and a lot of prayer. They'll need some
money to see them through until they get settled. Anyone who wants to
contribute, bring your money to the party."

"Let's all stand and close in prayer."

We went around the circle with each person taking a couple of
minutes to praise God for all that he was doing and asking for God's
protection over Frankie and me.

Life was about to take an exciting turn.

CHAPTER 56

The word spread quickly throughout the neighborhood. People came from all around the city to express their thanks for all that Young Life was doing.

Momentum was building rapidly toward the meeting on Wednesday night. Father Brown, one of the priests at St. Chris's, felt that his church might be too small for such a meeting, so he had contacted one of the schools. Together they arranged for us to use the cafeteria, which was a lot larger.

That night, people began arriving early. Even before the meeting was scheduled to start, the place was already overflowing.

We started off as usual with a lot of singing. Then Joey stood and talked about the coming events. When he had finished, he asked me to say a few words.

"You all have been so kind to me. I came here a stranger and you took me into your hearts. I also came here as a-know-it-all who thought only I had all the right answers. I saw myself as better than you because I had a high school education."

I paused for a moment. "I also saw myself as better than you because I was white. I saw myself as better than most because I felt that nobody was as close to God as I was. Well, in spite of my stupidity, arrogance, and selfishness, you loved me and treated me with a respect that I did not deserve. I also felt that I couldn't be my real self. I felt like I had to pretend to be Mr. Perfect, the good Christian, or else you wouldn't respect me."

Pausing again, I snickered and added, "Well, you know what I mean; after all, respect is what it is all about. If nobody respects you, you ain't anybody. Least that's what I thought.

"Over the past two weeks God has done a lot of work in my life. I am so thankful for the love of each of you, and especially for Carmen and her great love for me. I miss her very much."

I started to tear up this time; I did not try to stop the tears. She was so special to me. She was God's special angel to let me know that despite all my mistakes, God still loved me.

"One other thing I'd like to share with you is that God loves you, just as He loves me, just as we are. We don't need to change for God to love us. Once we ask God to come into our hearts and run our lives, He might show us some things that we need to change, but don't get all hung up on feeling like you got to do something special or follow a whole lot of rules, new rules, so as to please God.

"Just take that first step tonight and admit that you need God; admit that your life is empty, and that life has no meaning. Let Jesus show you how to really enjoy life. Thanks."

Jumping up from where he had been sitting, Frankie smiled broadly at me and then said in a very loud voice, "OK, Jim, have a seat—sit down. My turn now! Let's hear it for Jim."

The place erupted in a loud and thunderous roar of approval with clapping, foot stomping, whistling, and cheers.

"OK, OK—like I said, it's my turn." Frankie laughed loudly. He was having the time of his life.

"For years, I've been trying to understand how I could become a Christian. I wanted to, just like some of youse punks, but I just couldn't stay straight. One minute I was clean and the next, strung out again. Just couldn't let go of the drugs. Oh, I tried so many times. Just didn't work for me.

"One day last week, Joey was explaining to me that I didn't have to be clean or perfect before Jesus could come into my life. Fact was, I had already asked Jesus several times and he had heard me—funny.

"I just didn't know it. Well, now I know it. And after listening to Jim talk," he chuckled, "I'm a whole heck of a lot better Christian than he is."

Once again, everyone cheered. Frankie was a local boy, and everyone loved him.

"Well, tonight I've come to say goodbye to all of my friends. Tomorrow me and Jim leave for a new home—Chicago.

"Yeah, that's right. I hope to see my friend Vinny when we get there. Jim's going to Bible college, and me—well, I'm just going along for the adventure and to get away from youse punks."

Frankie held up his boney fingers in a victory sign: two fingers on each hand formed the letter V. A lot of cheering followed. Shuffling as he walked to his seat, Frankie grinned at the crowd.

Joey stood up and everyone got quiet. "You heard what they had to say. How many of you are tired of being alone?

"Being afraid of life?

"Wishing life could change for you?

"Hoping that somebody somewhere really cared if you lived or died?

"Jesus cares. If you want Jesus to come into your life and show you how much he loves you; if you want what God has to offer, and you yearn for some peace in your life, stand up now and raise your hand."

Kids from all over the room stood and raised their hands. Suddenly a lot of crying could be heard.

"Let us pray," Joey said. "Jesus, give these people a chance. Come into their hearts and make them new people—people filled with your love and mercy. Help them to feel loved by you. Help us to love them, in Jesus's name, amen."

We spent the next two hours talking in groups of four with those who had raised their hands. Thank God we had all the staff there. So many lives were changed that night.

Tomorrow Frankie and I would get on a train and leave for Chicago. Little did we know what a dangerous life we were heading into. We would be "jumping from the frying pan into the fire." Black Power and I would be arriving at the same time.

CHAPTER 57

Frankie and I headed back to our apartment. When we arrived, we noticed Benny's big black limo sitting out front. My mind raced.

Why is Benny here? Did Frankie do something wrong? Are we about to get hurt?

Out of the corner of my eye, I could see Frankie shuffling nervously, dragging his left foot. Turning his head toward me, I sensed fear in his eyes. Suddenly one of the passenger doors burst open and out jumped one of Benny's thugs.

"Get in the car, you two—now!"

I stepped in first, followed by Frankie. Darkness filled the inside. A small shaft of light penetrated through the window behind the driver

A strong smell of fresh cigar smoke told me that Benny was in the darkness somewhere. It's a good thing it was so dark, as it prevented Benny from seeing the panicked look of fear in my eyes.

Never in my wildest dreams did I expect that my adventure in New York would once again be threatened with such a violent end.

Assuming that Benny was in his usual spot, I felt my way along the seat on my right. It was such a big and roomy car. I quickly moved over to the far end opposite Benny and sat down.

"**Drive**," Benny growled

We rode in silence for about twenty minutes. My mind was racing with fears.

Glancing over at Frankie, I could see he was very nervous.

We turned down a street and headed toward the river.

Should I attempt to escape? Could we overpower Benny and the guy sitting next to me?

Are we about to die—again?

Suddenly my thoughts were shattered and my heart almost stopped beating.

"Stop the car here," Bennie growled.

Well, this was it. I felt sorry for Frankie, really sorry, because he was on the verge of realizing his dream come true: leaving the city and making a new life for himself. Well, at least in a few minutes we would both be leaving this city for a new life with Jesus.

When the car came to a complete stop, Benny leaned forward and turned on the light. I could see that his face had a very troubled look on it.

"I've been watching you guys. Heard about tonight's meeting. Is it true you two are leaving tomorrow for Chicago?"

Stunned, I said, "Yeah, Frankie and I leave in the morning. Soon be out of your hair."

Frankie grunted a laugh.

Leaning back, Benny took out a cigar box, opened it, and offered us both a cigar.

We both shook our heads no.

Benny took his time picking out just the right cigar.

Then, after moistening it and biting off an end, he slowly lit his cigar.

Quietly he took a couple of slow puffs. Then, leaning forward, he eyed each of us again.

"Jim, I know how much you loved Carmen. I've watched how much you've suffered. I can't say I know how you feel or how much you hurt—only you and God know that. I've never really loved anyone, except myself.

"I've been watching you...Eddie...Frankie...and Joey. I want that kind of love in my life that has changed these guys and allowed you to continue in spite of what happened to Carmen."

"I want to learn how to love someone else. I want to be loved, not just feared.

"Secondly, no one will ever have to worry about Ricky and his brothers. They're being taken care of as we speak."

Thank God for that.

Bennie sat back and smiled. His smile disappeared and he got a real serious look in his eyes.

"Why, Jim—why were you willing to die for Frankie?"

Bennie searched my eyes carefully.

"And Eddie, no one makes a fool out of Eddie the way you did. Why do you do these things?"

He shifted in his seat.

"No one's ever done anything like that for me."

His head hung down.

No one said anything. The silence was frightening.

"I don't understand you...don't understand Joey...don't understand any of you."

Slowly he shook his head

"Tell me, fellas," he said with tears in his voice, "*what do I need to do to have Jesus in my life?*"

CONCLUSION

This story is based on true events that I lived through. I fully believe that God has guided me to write this story. Many of the thoughts, prayers, and words came from Him. All glory to God for His constant protection over me during those years.

Frankie and I went on to Moody Bible College in Chicago where I became a student and he worked on the maintenance staff. We saw each other every day.

I started a ministry for Young Life there working with a gang deep in the violent territory that was run by the Blackstone Rangers. It was an extremely dangerous time in my life, with many more opportunities for God to prove Himself faithful in protecting me.

My next book will be centered on a girl named Joyce, a particularly violent girl gang leader, who found out that surrendering her life to Jesus would lead to her death in such a violent world.

Great is thy faithfulness, O God my Father
Morning by morning new mercies I see;
All I have needed Thy hand hath provided
Great is thy faithfulness, Lord unto me.
Pardon for sin and a peace that endureth
Thy own dear presence to cheer and to guide
Strength for today and bright hope for tomorrow
Blessings all mine with ten thousand beside!
Great is thy faithfulness, O God my Father
Morning by morning new mercies I see;
All I have needed Thy hand has provided
Great is thy faithfulness, Lord, unto me.

One of the most common factors I discovered is that these youth who are violent come from homes where they do not feel loved by their fathers and **MOST OF ALL DO NOT FEEL VALUED**. They feel worthless. They then go out in search of both love and acceptance and most of all being valued. In the gangs they find these values. If we are to save America's youth, we must find a way to teach men to value their children both boys and girls.